Only i

'A funny and sweetly romantic
Daily Mail

'This book is the best thing to come out of Holland since tulips'
Harry Hill

'Short, smart and packed full of jokes, if this book wore glasses it would be Dominic Holland'
Nick Hancock

'Laugh out loud funny all over the place and absolutely screaming to be a film'
Mark Billingham, author of *Sleepyhead*

'A good read with a clever plot . . . the narrative is laced with musing on the minor perplexities of life'
Evening Standard

'His hilariously funny and sharply written novel is the type of light-hearted work you'd expect from such a comic'
Western Mail

'Witty and charming. Astonishingly good. Quite irritating in fact'
Angus Deayton

'The jokes flow slick and fast'
Glamour

'A fine stand-up comic has turned into a first class, laugh out loud novelist. Read and enjoy'
Barry Cryer

DOMINIC HOLLAND

ONLY IN AMERICA

FLAME
Hodder & Stoughton

Copyright © 2002 by Dominic Holland

First published in Great Britain in 2002 by Hodder and Stoughton
A division of Hodder Headline

The right of Dominic Holland to be identified as the Author
of the Work has been asserted by him in accordance with the
Copyright, Designs and Patents Act 1988.

A Flame paperback

5 7 9 10 8 6

A CIP catalogue record for this title is available from the British Library

ISBN 0 340 81986 3

Typeset in Sabon by Phoenix Typesetting, Burley-inWharfedale, West Yorkshire

Printed and bound in Great Britain by
Clays Ltd, St Ives plc

Hodder and Stoughton
A division of Hodder Headline
338 Euston Road
London NW1 3BH

For Tom, Sam and Harry

ACKNOWLEDGEMENTS

I would like to thank so many people at Hodder who have had a hand in getting *Only In America* off the ground: Carolyn Mays, Robert Williams, Hazel Orme and my publicist Sam Evans, but in particular Sara Hulse. Sara's encouragement and commitment to the book from its very early stages and throughout the writing process (and subsequent re-writes) has been astounding, and I am tremendously grateful to her. Thanks also go to both Al Oliver and Lucy Bennett for their great talent and efforts with the artwork for *Only In America*'s two covers and latterly to Mari Evans and Emma Longhurst.

I would like to thank my agents Jan Kennedy and Robert Kirby, and state for the record that the agent character in the novel was not in any way inspired by them. Thanks also for readings and support to my sister Sarah Povey and Liz Style. But my greatest thanks go to my wife, Nikki, who has helped with the script more than I care to admit. Indeed, some of the best ideas in the book are hers, and that is something I am struggling to come to terms with.

Only in America

CHAPTER ONE

At 6.15, Milly's alarm radio obediently came to life.

'. . . that was the latest single from Ireland's first family, the Corrs . . .'

She hit the snooze button. The only good thing about the morning so far was that she'd managed to miss the latest effort by the Corrs, another droning ballad no doubt, churned out by beautiful women singing inexplicably about not being loved. Reluctantly, she broke her heat chamber and poked a foot out from under the duvet and then snatched it back in again. It was bloody freezing. These days her radiators seemed to generate more noise than heat. She had a vague idea that some kind of bleeding was required, but of what and from where was a complete mystery to her.

Wrapped in a bath towel emblazoned with the words 'Shelton Tower, Park Lane', Milly hunted through her wardrobe for a blouse that was ironed, or at least one that she might be able to get away with. No such luck. She threw a blouse on the bed and retrieved her underwear from the top of the lukewarm radiator, putting it on as quickly as possible before rushing into her laundry room, or spare bedroom to give it its official title. The ironing board was permanently up, and she longed for the day when she didn't have an airer draped in clothes at varying degrees of dampness. As reception manager of the Shelton Tower, Park Lane, it just wasn't acceptable to turn up with a sticking-up collar. The rogue lapel seemed to laugh at her iron's cotton setting, but eventually submitted after an extended burst of steam.

In her kitchen, she filled the kettle with just enough water for one cup and threw a tea bag into her favourite mug. It had been her first present from Elliot and was all she had left to show for a marriage that had ended so traumatically for her four years ago. She and Elliot had fallen hopelessly in love and hadn't noticed that they were completely incompatible: she was a confirmed romantic and he a serial philanderer.

Breakfast today was a dull affair. She ruined her tea with too much milk and, living alone, she always got bored as she neared the end of a box of cereal. This morning even her Special K Red Berries were proving hard work.

'So it is going to be a wet one, London. A one hundred per cent chance of rain by this afternoon . . .' the effervescent disc jockey chirped.

Becoming increasingly irritated, Milly was searching for her umbrella. Her hall cupboard offered up piles of newspapers and bags of cans and bottles waiting to be recycled, but no umbrella. 'Shit. Where is it?' she moaned, carefully closing the door on the chaos once again. She checked her bedroom wardrobe for the second time. It still wasn't there, it hadn't materialised. 'Someone's nicked it,' she announced irrationally as she took a deep breath, as if that could possibly help. Suddenly, she remembered this afternoon's christening, and that she hadn't wrapped the blasted present. If a large golf umbrella was difficult to find, then what chance did she have with a roll of Sellotape?

After another five minutes of mostly repetitive searching, a thoroughly vanquished Milly sat at her desk. Wrapping paper festooned with snowmen and a roll of masking tape was the best she could do. And still no umbrella. With a hand massaging each temple, she sighed heavily. 'I have got to get more organised,' she said very slowly, as if it were the start of a more measured and exact direction to her life. 'It's as simple as that. This weekend, Saturday, it's a dump run and organising the flat.'

Her Tube journey from South Ealing into London was always painful. The Piccadilly line serves Heathrow airport, and so, as it crawls into the station, each train is already heavily laden with people spanning the globe, none of whom ever get off. No one flies three thousand miles to get off at South Ealing. She called it the grope hour, and this morning she travelled into town forced up against a backpack from Oz, a suitcase from Rio and a crotch from Hounslow.

Just before eight o'clock, a well-groomed Milly chased up the steps of the Shelton Tower, Park Lane. The door opened for her courtesy of Samson, the hotel's oldest and longest-serving employee.

'Morning, Milly. You look as lovely as ever.' He smiled.

'Thank you, Samson. Looks like rain today.'

'Let's hope so.' He chuckled. 'Rain. Rain. The more it tips, the more tips I get.'

Hotel doormen along with English cricketers playing Australia are possibly the only two professions that pray for rain.

The Shelton Tower hotel was truly a magnificent building. Built in the 1850s as London's most opulent office block, it had been converted into a hotel just after the First World War, and had put up the world's most privileged people ever since. As with most hotels, its reception area was its centrepiece. Huge marble staircases snaked down into it and forests of mahogany had been used to panel the walls, all hand carved and French polished. Light cascaded through an original stained-glass roof some one hundred feet above the marble mosaic floor. It was a hotel worthy of its five-star status and had no trouble attracting five-star guests.

Reception this morning was busy, but Milly could sense that something was awry. Luggage was accumulating at the concierge desk and a few esteemed guests (all the residents of the Shelton were esteemed) were looking flustered. Four clocks were positioned over the reception desk pointlessly displaying times around the world. On her last day at work, she planned to synchronise the times and change the signs to read London, Grimsby, Southend and Billericay. The London clock said it was just after eight.

'Morning, Lucas.'

'Boy. Am I glad to see you.'

'What's up?'

'Three bell-boys have bunked off. Mahmood's gone and done his nut.'

'Shit. But we're okay for this afternoon, yeah?'

4

'What do you mean?'

She tutted. 'Lucas. What we talked about. The christening.'

His smile gave him away, much to her relief. She and Lucas hadn't got off to a good start. First, she had been promoted to manager ahead of him, but worse still she had spurned all his romantic advances. It was hardly surprising. At twenty-five, he was seven years younger than her and frankly totally out of his depth. Fortunately, though, he was a graduate of the no-harm-in-asking academy, and they'd become good friends.

'So you're having the whole afternoon off?'

'Yes,' Milly replied tentatively.

'The whole afternoon?'

'Yeah.'

'And I'm covering for you?'

'Like we discussed. Yes.'

'Okay, then. But you're gonna owe me,' he said mischievously, pursing his lips. 'A whole afternoon off. That's gotta be worth at least . . .'

'Lucas.' She stopped him, raising her hand. 'Let's not go there, eh? Not yet anyway. It's too early.'

His whimsical smile was suddenly replaced with his highly efficient professional receptionist look, which could only mean that Mr Mahmood was approaching. Mr Mahmood was the Shelton's general manager, a fastidious Turk who quite simply lived for the hotel and the people it served. It was almost like a religion to him. His was a calling to serve rich people. At five feet one and a half, he felt the need to stand up so straight that in fact he leant backwards. His head was rigidly fixed forward with his arms stuck firmly to his sides, and he moved at incredible speed. He walked so quickly his little legs were almost a blur, and with his rigid upper body he reminded Milly of a swan, although he didn't have the murky water to disguise his efforts. Reception to Mr Mahmood acted like a speed camera, slowing him down sufficiently for him to engage in a very prompt conversation with his reception manager.

'Mill-ee. Everything is okay. Yess?'

Milly gave a regimental nod as he moved off, and fought her continual urge to salute, stamp her foot and scream, 'Sir. Yes, sir.' He had a habit of answering his own questions, and his determination to lose his Turkish accent meant that he had a tendency to over-enunciate his words.

As the morning progressed, Mr Mahmood became more and more angry. He was furious that the bell-boys had thought so little of their job that they'd decided not to come in. He couldn't conceive that they might have found better jobs elsewhere, because there was no better job than working at the Shelton Tower. Granted, it was highly suspicious that all three had been taken ill on the same day, but it wouldn't have mattered if they had genuinely been at death's door. They might have had rabies and he would still have expected them. Luggage being delivered by frothing Puerto Ricans was better than no luggage delivered at all. As ever, setting the standard, Mr Mahmood and his assistant had been trying to reduce the gathering luggage mountain that would soon warrant its own chair lift. Since he had left on his last baggage run, the Buffalo Bills had arrived at the hotel. They were in

London for a promotional game to prove once and for all that American football would never take off outside the States. Forty-three gargantuan gentlemen, each with luggage the size of a family car that was now being piled high in the reception area. One vast and gruesome-looking player wearing a headscarf took an instant and uncomfortable shine to Milly.

'Hey, Rudy,' he said to one of his mates, 'I think Milly here looks even better than some of our cheerleaders.'

A few Buffalos looked over and snorted their agreement, marvelling at the brass neck of their colleague.

'Can you high-kick, Milly?'

She smiled. Just about high enough to bring a tear to your eye, she thought.

'Would you like to be a cheerleader?' the ath-a-lete asked.

'Do you really think I could make it?' she gasped, as doe-eyed as a Disney heroine.

'Sure you could.' Despite his enormous height, her irony had passed straight over him. 'I could put in a word for you. If you know what I mean.'

'Er, no thanks.' She didn't know much about American football, but she suspected that this guy was probably a member of Offense.

'I love it here. They told me that little old Eng-land has some of the most beautiful women in the world. Oh, yeah. And I tell ya. They ain't bin lyin'.'

'Thank you.' She blushed, feeling ridiculous for saying it.

'I like it here. Being somewhere where I don't get mobbed all the time for signings and photos.'

'Really? Well, in that case, I think you're going to love it here,' she said, comfortable that he wouldn't get what she meant.

'I'm sure I will.' The Buffalo leant his considerable frame on the desk and bent in for a more intimate moment. He was probably scraping his right foot back and forth in readiness to charge. He held up his key-card.

'Hell, I'm already having a great time. You know the number. You feel free to run yourself off a copy whenever you like. So, I guess I'll be seeing you later, then.'

'Yes, you will.'

A cheer from the herd. Touchdown! Good old Marvin. Scored before he'd even got to his room. A new Buffalos record!

'When you check out.' She added, and this time he got it. All 280 pounds of solid athletic muscle, winded by an eight-stone receptionist.

The service lift arrived. Its doors opened and two empty luggage trolleys appeared, pushed by a weary-looking, crimson-faced Mr Mahmood. The sight that greeted him was appalling. There was a queue at Reception and he could no longer see the concierge desk, or even Hyde Park. Two of his five gold stars from the hotel sign were metaphorically lying on the exquisite marble floor. He shot Lucas a gruesome look. He hadn't done anything wrong, but someone had to be shouted at.

'Lucass. A wordd, pliss?' he barked through gritted teeth as he scuttled into the back office beyond Reception, with the unfortunate Lucas trundling after him in his slipstream. The demented manager was waiting impatiently as Lucas shut the door behind him.

'Lucass. Pliss explen t'mee. What the faking hell is going on in my hotel?' His accent was always more acute when he was angry. Sadly for Lucas, this wasn't one of his rhetorical questions.

'Well. The bell-boys are sick and . . .'

'I know that,' he screamed, shaking his head around as if he were being pestered by a wasp. 'Lucass. Lookk at me. Lookk at my face.'

'Yes, sir.'

'Do I look like an idiot?'

Lucas grimaced. 'No, sir.'

'I'm sweating like a faking pigge. I know they're sickk. No. They're not sickk. Faking skiving bastardes. But they will be, if they ever show up at my hotel . . .'

He stopped mid-rant as the door opened, and Milly's head appeared. ('The hotel reception is never to be left unmanned.')

'There'll be a queue past the Hilton shortly,' was all she said. Without another word, the little moustachioed inferno swept past and ushered Milly out before him. He marched straight up to the next guest at the desk.

'Mr Sakamoto.' He did a reverent Japanese-style bow before the startled-looking guest. 'Welcome back to the Shelton Tower, Park Lane. My humblest apologies for the delay.'

Welcome back? The man looked increasingly confused. 'I am not Mr Sakamoto.'

There was an awkward silence as Mr Mahmood fumbled for an explanation. 'You're not?' he asked. Perhaps the gentleman was jet-lagged and had forgotten his own name.

'No,' the man replied resolutely. He was quite sure that he wasn't Mr Sakamoto.

'I amm so sorry.' Mr Mahmood floundered for something more substantial to say. But all that came to mind was hideous. 'Oh, well, easy mistake to make, eh? I mean, you little Japanese fellahs, you all look so alike.'

Milly speedily consulted her computer and saved Mr Mahmood's blushes. 'My mistake. This is Mr Konishi. I am sorry for the confusion. Mr Sakamoto has already checked in.'

The guest smiled at the simple explanation and a relieved looking Mr Mahmood congratulated himself on his decision to make Milly his reception manager.

'Thank you, Mr Povey. I'm glad that you enjoyed your stay and we look forward to being able to serve you again,' Milly said. Another business gladiator refreshed and ready to face his day filled with breaded crustaceans and chilled Chardonnay. Milly didn't really notice what the guests actually did for a living. They were all president of this, chairman of that. Being a captain of industry didn't really do it for her. Granted, their company might well have a zillion-dollar turnover, but that was usually dependent on something as mundane as Joe Schmo choosing to wipe his arse with their toilet paper. As far as the guests were concerned, it was only the celebrities who really caught Milly's eye, but, as a seasoned hotel professional, she was increasingly difficult to impress. These days, the word 'star' is used far too casually, she thought, soap star being a case in point, a contradiction in terms, surely. Thankfully, though, the Shelton attracted more than its quota of A-list celebrities, and no matter how rude or aloof they were, they always lifted the staff's morale. Mr Clint Eastwood was currently in residence, but anyone associated with Hollywood interested Milly. After her marriage collapsed, so did Milly – as did her career as a buyer. Her mother called it a career break, but it was a nervous breakdown, and Milly couldn't see that it was anything to be ashamed of. She took the job at the hotel as a temporary measure, and set about turning her lifelong hobby of creative writing into a professional career as a screenwriter, no less. Her first screenplay, *Artistic Licence*, had been a resounding success. It won a prestigious *Daily Telegraph* screenplay competition and secured Milly the services of ILM, London's premier literary agency. Milly was flying. The script was then bought by Paramount Studios, although she never did actually receive any of the money before they lost interest altogether. However, she liked to think that the script was sold; it sounded so much better than saying it had been borrowed for a while. It was a wildly exciting time for her, but sadly since then things had slowed drastically. *Artistic Licence* was now dead, and it appeared that her agent, Lyal Roberts, wished she was too. He had had her latest screenplay, *Untitled*, for over four months now, and still she hadn't heard from him. At great expense, which she could ill afford, Milly had attended two screenwriting courses, and the resounding message from them both was: *Do whatever it takes to get your script into the decision-maker's hands*. The hotel had presented her with some wonderful opportunities. Spielberg, the Coen brothers, Coppola, Katzenberg, they'd all stayed at the Shelton, but sadly she hadn't managed to trouble any of them. A number of Hollywood luminaries were in Mr Eastwood's party, including Albert T. Willenheim, the infamous film mogul who currently headed up Pacific Studios. They didn't come any bigger than that, Milly thought. Ambitious young writers the world over would kill for access to Albert T. Willenheim, and yet Milly feared that he would be added to her growing list of missed opportunities. She had lots of reasons to explain her inaction, but none of them stood up to much scrutiny. They ranged from: 'They won't read it anyway' to 'It's against hotel policy to solicit a guest with anything other than first-rate service'. This was of course nonsense. Theft was also strictly against hotel policy, and she hadn't bought linen or towels for years. The truth was that she was terrified of these people and terrified of being rejected, and had decided that she would do nothing but believe passionately in fate. All those years at school learning about algebra and ox-bow lakes and not one lesson in self-esteem! And anyway, just what the hell would she say to someone like Albert T. Willenheim?

'Mr Willenheim, welcome back to the Shelton Tower. How was your day today? I trust your meeting with Mr Caine was a success. He's one of our best actors. Ignore Jaws III *it was just a blip. Now, let's see, you have many urgent messages, but never mind them for the moment. Here's my latest screenplay which I want you to read this afternoon 'cos I'm not in tomorrow . . .'*

It was now just after ten o'clock and Reception was finally quietening down after the morning rush. The luggage mountain was no longer snow capped and an air of serenity reigned, for the moment at least.

'Milly. That movie guy's in having breakfast,' Lucas said casually.

'Yeah. I saw them all go in.'

'So, you gonna go for it or what?'

'Have you been speaking to Georgina?'

'No. Why?' he said defensively.

''Cos you sound just like her.'

Increasingly, most of her friends seemed keen that she should humiliate herself in front of a Hollywood executive, and chief among them was her best friend Georgina. She'd spent most of the previous evening explaining why Milly should just accept that her agent was a useless little shit and that she had to 'empower herself and become proactive'. Georgina was in PR. She'd pressed for a full movie pitch, which was rejected, but Milly did concede that she should at least introduce herself. As Georgina had said over and over *ad nauseam*, Milly had nothing to lose, apart from her dignity, of course.

'So. What about it?' Lucas asked again.

'Oh, I don't know.'

'Why not? You've got nothing to lose.'

Milly looked at him suspiciously.

'And you haven't spoken to Georgina?'

'No. I swear. I just think you should do something about it. That's all.'

'What? Just like that, eh?'

'I'm not saying how, that's your department. It's just that he's staying here and you *have* got a key to his room.' Another Georgina line.

'You bloody have spoken to her.'

Lucas wasn't worried about being found out because something over Milly's shoulder distracted him.

'Shit, Milly. Over by the lifts. Don't look. Don't look.'

'What?'

'Clint Eastwood.'

The film star hadn't been seen in the hotel since he'd arrived. Mr Eastwood wasn't so much a star, more a planet, and planets can visit hotels with no one knowing. They don't check themselves in, and they don't use any communal areas, preferring to hole up in their suites with their assistants and room service.

'Yes,' Lucas muttered under his breath. 'He's coming over.'

The actor ambled over to the desk, and although Lucas was the first receptionist he came to he continued walking until he stood face to face with Milly. Lucas was as gutted as Milly was flattered.

'Ma'am,' he said politely, as his piercing eyes held her gaze.

'Yes, sir. How can I help?' Milly smiled. She had a beautiful smile, which lit up her already animated face. It wasn't lost on the famous guest.

'I seem to have misplaced my key-card. Would you be able to get me another one?'

'No problem, Mr Eastwood. It would be my pleasure. Normally I'd need ID, but I don't think in this instance I'll bother. Somehow you look familiar to me.'

Mr Eastwood laughed and she was delighted.

'Maybe it's because I've stayed here before,' he said, continuing her theme.

'Yes. That must be it.' She handed him the key-card.

'Thank you very much, Milly.'

'You're welcome,' she fluttered as he nodded and took his leave. She wondered whether he ever got bored with making people's days. Normally she had to content herself with celebrities that she had just seen, but this was altogether different. With Mr Eastwood, she'd spoken to him, made him laugh and he had called her Milly. That saw him go straight in at number one in her anecdote charts.

'I'll have to report that to Mr Mahmood,' Lucas said indignantly.

'What?'

'What do you mean, what? Flirting with guests.'

'I didn't flirt with him.'

'Yeah, right.'

'Ah, so what.'

'So. If you can hit on Clint Eastwood, I don't see why you can't introduce yourself to that Willen ... er, Will ...'

'Will-en-heim,' Milly helped him, although she wished she could help herself. From the safety of her own bedroom, she'd made Internet searches on all the members of the Eastwood party, apart from Mr Willenheim. The only one to register anything was Mitch Carmichael, head of development at Pacific. As such, he was the man she should be approaching. In fact he was very approachable indeed, something she instantly regretted telling Georgina. Mr Carmichael always looked distracted and stressed, something with which Milly could empathise and for which she liked him, but that didn't mean she was about to break her duck.

'The opening of your screenplay is the only bit they're

definitely going to read, so make sure it grabs their attention.' Another of the great mantras from the screenwriting courses she'd attended. On the Underground this morning, Milly had wondered whether the opening of her screenplay met this crucial criterion. It was definitely funny, no doubt about that, but was it a grabber? Would it compel the reader to read on? Possibly not, and so she concluded that perhaps it wasn't the best time to pitch it or herself to one of the biggest film producers in the world. How convenient for her!

'Speak of the devil.' Lucas gestured over to the breakfast lounge.

Willenheim could be heard before he emerged, his mighty frame filling the entrance to the lounge, with his entourage in close attendance. He looked bloated, as if he'd just pulled his chair up to the breakfast buffet to save his legs. Indeed, he was still finishing his 'full English' while barking and spitting orders. His sheer size, his reputation, his job, whatever it was, he had an air of 'Don't fuck with me'. Not even Mr Mahmood had introduced himself to this particular guest, which was probably just as well.

'I don't give a rat's ass,' Willenheim boomed, and walked across the lobby towards the lift. He still had his breakfast serviette tucked into his shirt, and he ripped it off, casting it over his shoulder into the hands of an assistant as if it were a bouquet at a wedding. Abruptly, he turned and pointed his fat index finger at a female assistant.

'I don't care what time it is in LA. Get his lazy ass out of bed.' The assistant looked as if she'd been hit by a water cannon, and other guests in the lobby shifted awkwardly. Willenheim glanced over at Reception and caught Milly's eye. He scowled. Georgina could stuff her ethos up her arse. There was no way in the world Milly was ever going to introduce herself to this guy. Willenheim and his entourage disappeared into the lift, but Mitch Carmichael was suddenly striding in her direction. Her back stiffened and she busied herself, trying to calm her nerves. 'Bollocks. Bollocks. Bollocks. This is it?'

The words 'THIS IS YOUR CHANCE' reverberated in her head, growing louder with each step he took.

'Hi,' he said casually.

'Can I help you, Mr Carmichael?'

He seemed startled that she should know his name. She hadn't checked him in and they'd not met, and Milly immediately worried about how she could explain it. It wouldn't be easy. *'It's nothing weird or anything. I just did an Internet search on you, that's all'* or *'Last night, me and a mate were talking about how cute you were. I said that you reminded me of a young Harrison Ford and that you'd look great with a whip.'*

'Are there any messages for Mr Willenheim?' he asked.

She knew there weren't, but she began searching anyway to extend her window of opportunity sufficiently for her to possibly take the plunge.

'Are you enjoying your stay?'

MILLY, THIS IS YOUR CHANCE.

'Erm, er, yes. Thank you,' he replied. He didn't seem to be in the mood for trite small talk.

'Business trip?'

'Er, yes.'

NEVER MIND SMALL TALK. HE'S A BUSY MAN. JUST GET TO THE POINT.

'Busy, is it?' she asked feebly. Desperate to keep the conversation alive and yet acutely aware that she wasn't exactly dazzling him with her charm.

'A little fraught,' he replied, somewhat curtly now.

'Oh?' Milly persevered.

He forced a smile. 'Yeah. You know. Business is a little tough right now. Sometimes I wish I had a job with no responsibility.'

'I know how that feels,' Milly said.

'Oh, no. I wasn't meaning . . .'

'Don't worry,' she reassured him. 'What business are you in?'

'Movies.' He sounded slightly embarrassed.

OKAY. THIS IS MY MOMENT. TAKE IT. TAKE IT NOW.

'Wow. That must be exciting.'

WHAT WAS THAT? I CAN'T BELIEVE I SAID THAT.

'Yeah, I guess.'

Milly's heart was pounding so hard now, that she wondered whether he might notice it trying to burst out of her chest.

JUST TELL HIM THAT YOU'VE WRITTEN A FUCKING FILM, WILL YOU.

'Erm, I love films,' she whimpered.

'You do? That's great. Okay . . . so, are there any messages?'

His question jolted her.

18

'Er, no. No, sorry. No messages.'

'Okay. I'm glad we finally got that straight. Nice talking with you.' He turned and left. Ineptitude on such a grand scale. What a woeful performance.

Typically, she instantly began trying to convince herself that the moment had been all wrong. The timing wasn't right. But it was futile. Right there! That had just been her golden opportunity, wheeled over on a splendid dessert trolley under one of those magnificent silver salvers, and had she taken it? Had she hell.

No thank you. Not for me. Just a black coffee, please. Georgina would go mad.

CHAPTER TWO

The christening Milly was attending was that of Jonson Clarke's niece. Jonson was her oldest friend. Their families had been neighbours for years, until Milly's had moved 'up the ladder', as her mother put it.

As her train drew into Lewisham station, thunder crashed and rain fell in torrents. Milly berated herself for having failed to borrow an umbrella from work. Outside the station, people huddled under cover, timing their exit to coincide with the arrival of buses and taxis. Others seemed content to wait it out. Better late than wet. Milly, though, didn't have the luxury of time: she hitched up the collar of her wool jacket and leapt out into the downpour.

She entered the porch of St Edmund's Church at exactly three o'clock. She was soaked, so she peeled off her sodden coat. The porch floor was covered with puddles from the umbrellas that had been left there to dry, all different shapes and colours, and in varying states of disrepair. Some were in a very sorry state and had most likely seen their last ever action today. The one that particularly caught her eye was hers. She realised at once how it had got there. Jonson had been at her flat a week ago and it had been raining. He had refused her offer of a lift and must have settled for nicking her umbrella.

Her mother, Margaret, had arrived and came to meet her. 'Juliet! You're wet through, dear.'

Only her family called her Juliet – 'Milly' was a school nickname. 'Juliet Millhouse' had presented many possibilities but Milly was the one that had stuck.

'Honestly,' Margaret went on, 'haven't you got an umbrella?'

'Yes, Mum, I have, but I couldn't find it. Where's Dad?'

'Parking the car. What do you mean, you couldn't find it? Why don't you leave it by your front door? Honestly, Juliet, you simply have to get—'

'Organised. I know.'

Mercifully Margaret spotted an old neighbour. 'Oh, look, it's Marjorie. Gosh, hasn't she aged? I must pop over and say hello.'

Milly sighed. This was the sort of day her mum lived for. It was a chance to tell her friends of yesteryear how well they had been doing since Howard had started his business . . .

Milly looked around the church with affection. She'd been baptised and made her first Holy Communion here and discovered that she had a problem with confidence and public speaking. She'd had to say a prayer in front of her school and all the parents, but she'd frozen: her brain had steadfastly refused to connect her memory with her tongue.

Today at St Edmund's she had encountered a scene typical of the exuberant West Indian Clarke family. Mrs Clarke was a larger-than-life matriarch. Today she'd had her hair done specially and was wearing a shocking pink outfit. At least two sizes too small, the jacket buttons looked to be under enormous strain and must have been sewn on with wire.

The chattering and laughter among them all were deafening, but above it Mrs Clarke could be heard organising her chaotic family.

Milly had loved living next door to the Clarkes. She was an only child and the Clarke boys practically became her brothers, and she was as close as ever to Jonson. Like Milly's, Jonson's job was supposed to be a stopgap. At the moment he worked as one of London's intrepid cycle couriers but he still had lofty aspirations of becoming famous. He'd made countless television appearances as an extra, and had even secured a role as a principal extra in *Braveheart* until someone had pointed out that Scotland hadn't had any marauding black men in the fourteenth century. He had had his closest brush with fame in a Colgate commercial but, much to his consternation, only his smile eventually featured in it.

When Mrs Clarke spotted Milly, she immediately stopped what she was doing and bounded over to her. 'Milly, ma gurl,' she squealed, and crushed Milly to her ample breasts. 'You lookin' gorgeous, gurl.'

'Thanks, Mrs C. You look great yourself.'

'I know dat, dear,' she said, and brushed her hands admiringly down her curvaceous figure. 'I've bin and joined a gym.'

Milly wasn't sure whether this was a joke until Mrs Clarke's head fell back and she shrieked with laughter.

'Oh, I don't know, Mrs C, I could see you on a running machine.'

'Only if it was unplugged.'

'Or perhaps on a downhill setting,' Milly joked.

Mrs C roared. 'Da only ting I run now is ma reprobate family.'

Milly looked around at the pandemonium in the church. 'Well then, you should be as fit as a fiddle.'

Mrs Clarke's chubby hand clamped itself on to one of Milly's cheeks and shook it lovingly, although it still hurt. 'You still as cheeky as ever. You got a fellah yet?'

Milly shook her head.

'Wot is wrong wit men tooday? None a ma bwoys can settle wit one woman. Your 'usband,' she wagged her finger, ''e's an idiot. He come back cryin' won day . . . and you don' give 'im anodder chance. You give 'im a slap.'

A sheepish-looking Jonson sidled up to them. 'Hey, Milly, how are you doing?' He hugged her.

'Fine, if a little wet . . .' Milly was staring up at his hair. It always made an impression, but today . . .

'Hmm? Jonson. Your 'air look ridiculos, bwoy. Com' here,' Mrs C hollered, and waved a comb in his direction, which he instinctively avoided like a boxer. Luckily for him, at that moment she spotted Margaret. 'Milly, take dis comb and sort 'im out.'

Milly waited until Mrs Clarke had moved away, then put the comb in her bag. 'Sorry, Jonson, but your mum's right. What's happened to your hair?'

Jonson was famous for his hair. The world over, cool black guys had decided that the best thing to have on their heads was either nothing or almost nothing. Jonson didn't like the idea of black baldness. It gave tacit support to the idea that black people had hair that presented them with styling problems. So Jonson had lots of hair. The Jackson Five had crew cuts to Jonson's Afro. But today it was bigger than ever and it was glistening in a particularly unfashionable disco-like way.

'I stayed at Mum's last night,' Jonson explained. 'She was worried about me being late. You know what she's like.'

'Yeah. And?'

'Forgot me mousse, didn't I? Used some old stuff I found at Mum's. Must have been Dad's. No wonder he left it.' He touched his hair gingerly.

'Why didn't you wash it off?'

'I was about to, but Mum dragged me out the house. We've been here since one o'clock.'

Milly chuckled. Jonson always made her laugh. He didn't mean to; incredible and fantastic things just seemed to happen to him, most of which appeared prominently in her fiction. To a fledgling writer, Jonson was a literary gold mine, and she loved him for it. The opening scene of her current screenplay, the one that she now wanted to change, had been provided courtesy of Jonson. Surely he was the only person ever to be admitted to Hammersmith Hospital with boating injuries. He blamed the magnificent breasts of the wonderbra girl on an enormous billboard waiting to take men unawares as they headed off from the Broadway. Needless to say, Jonson was transfixed, like a moth to a lamp, and he and his bike failed to avoid the eighty-foot catamaran on its way to the Earl's Court Boat Show.

A drop of water flew off her hair and on to her

nose. She made a point of wiping it away so that Jonson noticed.

'Sorry about your brolly, mate. I took it the last time I was at yours,' he said.

'So I saw.' Her eyes were on his hair again. 'Still, I don't look as wet as you do.'

He chuckled shamefacedly and, unable to meet her eye, glanced around the church.

'I haven't been here since we left school,' she said.

'Yeah? Well, I have.'

'How come?'

'I've only been to confession, haven't I?'

'You haven't!' Milly cackled. The thought of Jonson confessing his sins to their ex-headmaster, Father Connolly, was too much for her.

'Mum made me. I'm one of the godparents, aren't I?'

'Oh, no.'

'It was awful . . . First thing he asked me?'

Milly thought for a moment. 'Dunno. What's with the hair?'

'When was my last confession?' Jonson tutted.

'Oh dear. When was it?' Milly asked.

'When we got confirmed. Twenty years ago, man.'

'Did you tell him that?'

'No. 'Course I didn't. Told him five years ago.'

'What? So you lied in confession?'

'Yeah. But I was about to admit to lying anyway,' he said, rather pleased with himself.

'Hi, guys.' It was Georgina, with her husband David beside her. Georgina had met Jonson through Milly, and now he and David played for the same football team. The four greeted each other with handshakes and kisses. Then Georgina turned to Milly.

'Well?' she asked.

'Well what?' Milly replied, although she knew exactly what her friend meant.

'Did we speak to our Hollywood moguls? As we discussed?'

'Oh . . . Yes. Actually I did.'

'Milly, that's *fantastic*. What happened?'

'Spoke with Mitch Carmichael.'

'Come on, come on, what did you talk about?'

'Oh, you know. Film and stuff.'

'Did you tell him about your script?'

'Yes,' she lied. 'He's given me an address in LA to send it to.'

'I *told* you, didn't I? And I bet you feel *great* about it.'

Milly managed a nod.

'And what about the romantic side of things?'

Milly tutted. Was there no pleasing this woman? 'Romance. Oh yeah, I forgot.'

'No, seriously.'

'Yeah. Absolutely . . . He proposed, actually.'

Georgina rolled her eyes.

'Yeah, just like that. He must have noticed I didn't have a ring and thought, What the hell? Nothing to lose. 'Course, I said yes. We're getting married later today. You can make it, can't you?'

At 3.20 Father Connolly called the proceedings to order. Family and friends crammed themselves into the first few pews while the parents and godparents assembled at the altar. The godmother was a very attractive young woman, and Jonson was thrilled at the prospect of them becoming related to each other, albeit in a godparent capacity.

'Jonson Clarke, hi,' he said, smiling at her and holding out his hand.

'Er Claire, Claire Gorard,' she replied, staring at his hair.

'It doesn't normally look like this,' he began, 'only I stayed at my mum's last night, and, well . . .' He petered out, realising that his explanation wasn't furthering his romantic cause.

Now, with the relevant people standing at the altar, Father Connolly was about to begin, when Mrs Clarke saw one of her many grandchildren trying to prise open a wall-mounted collection box for the poor. She picked him up and plonked him in Jonson's arms. Young Ben was a considerable weight but Jonson didn't want Claire to see that the child might be a struggle for him. It was all part of his mating advance towards her: stags clash horns and blokes can stand statue still while holding quite heavy children. It was also an opportunity to display his calming and authoritative way with children to the possible future mother of his own.

'In the name of the Father and of the Son and of the Holy Spirit,' Father Connolly began.

'Amen,' everyone muttered.

'Uncle Jonson, why is your hair like that?' the child asked loudly.

Jonson's eyes widened.

'Uncle Jonson.'

'Sshh,' he pleaded, hoping people might not have heard.

'If my hair looked like that, I would get it cut,' Ben added.

Jonson forced himself to smile. By now it was obvious that everyone had heard the brat's announcements. All heads were bowed, but not in prayer. Gently shaking shoulders and the odd snort were proof of that. Jonson shook his head in indignation. He'd had enough. He was now resolved to having his hair cut once and for all. Some other mug would have to carry the baton for Afro-Caribbean hair rights from now on.

'Let us pray,' said Father Connolly sternly.

'Yuk. It's all sticky, Uncle Jonson.'

Laughter, like wind, cannot be contained for long. It can be postponed but never abandoned, and indeed, often its intensity is only increased by a postponement. With Ben's latest timely revelation, another snaking crack appeared in the dam wall barely holding back the torrent of hysteria. To their credit, Jonson's family were all fighting it. Biting their lips, and gripping any available apparel, their eyes clamped shut, they were no doubt trying to imagine something sombre. They were all valiantly fighting a losing battle. Because it is a fact of life that the curiosity of smell always follows the sense of touch, the child then put his offending fingers to his nose and announced, 'Ehr, it stinks.'

With this, the dam burst open and the church was engulfed in a wave of uncontrollable laughter. Jonson looked on forlornly as his loved ones collapsed around him. They were all at it. Even Claire, the godmother, his godwife had lost it. Milly had been at funerals with fewer tears. And it seemed one might be needed as everyone heaved for air and clutched their chests. Eventually Father Connolly appealed for calm, and order eventually almost reasserted itself. In a bid to distract Ben, the priest gave the child a long thin candle to hold and lit it. 'Now, young Ben, do you know what this flame is?'

'A candle!'

'Yes. But it's a special candle. That flame is the light of Jesus, the light you received when you were baptised.'

Ben clutched the candle and immediately began trying to blow it out. 'Stop trying to blow Jesus out, Ben.' Now it was Jonson's turn to speak loudly, and soon he would wish that he hadn't. The child put his arm around his uncle's neck and the 'light of Jesus' promptly set fire to Jonson's incredibly large and incredibly combustible head, which lit up like an Olympic flame. It seemed an age before Jonson realised that he was actually on fire. Indeed, it was the congregation's reactions and appropriate cries of 'Jesus' that first alerted him to the idea that something wasn't quite right. Whatever it was, it had to be something big. The Second Coming even. He half expected to turn round and high-five the big fellah whilst apologising for not coming clean about all his sexual sins earlier.

As a kid, he'd burnt bits of his hair and loved the smell, but he was about to discover that it wasn't such a great smell when the hair that's burning is still attached to your head.

The pain wasn't far behind the smell and finally Jonson reacted. He dropped Ben and tore across to the font leaving a vapor trail in his wake. There was no time for pleasantries – *'Excuse me, Father Connolly, would you mind awfully if I interrupted your baptism? only it appears that my head is on fire.*' All he said was, 'Every-one, get out the fucking way', before he plunged into the font head first. The flames fizzled and went out. Smoke billowed about his shoulders. The church was now in a stunned silence, broken only by Jonson's whimpers. The family looked on bewildered. Had Jonson's head really caught fire?

Father Connolly spoke first. 'Are you okay, son?'

A strained moment passed before Jonson managed a thumbs-up, and a tidal wave of guffawing swept through the building. Sides ached and chests heaved as everyone lost control again. Jonson's younger brother Clinton yelped as a button exploded off Mrs C's jacket, catching him flush on the ear, but he still managed to keep videoing the whole thing. Maybe *You've Been Framed* might dedi-cate a whole show to his unfortunate brother.

Jonson insisted on staying in the font until the ambu-lance arrived, always assuming that someone had had the good heart and compassion to actually call one. He was going to live, but he knew that he would never live it down. People's conversation around the font had moved from Jonson's condition to whether, in all the commotion, the baby had been baptised or not. 'One thing's certain,' he heard someone say, 'Jonson definitely has been.'

Looking over at her dear friend dangling unceremoni-ously upside down, Milly felt a growing sense of guilt and shame. Of course she was concerned for Jonson but also she couldn't help smiling at her good fortune. Unwittingly, as ever, he had just provided her with a sensational 'grab 'em' scene to open her screenplay, and she couldn't wait to get home.

*   *   *

At 11.15 that night, Milly proudly hit the 'save' button on her PC with the christening scene complete. It was four and a half pages long, which would equate to as many screen minutes – and so another film law had been broken: *Your opening scene may not be any longer than four minutes.* It was a rule that *Saving Private Ryan* had ignored of course but rules no longer applied to Mr Spielberg.

She checked that her paper tray was full before nervously asking her printer whether it felt up to working today. It never printed anything without a protest, and her sympathetic PC would passively roll over and inform her that an 'unknown error' had been found. It was appropriate enough, though, and it amused Milly that her scripts should falter at such an early stage, even before anyone got to read them.

First thing tomorrow she would call her literary agent, Lyal Roberts, and explain that a new draft of her latest screenplay was on its way. He'd had the previous draft for four months now, and she hadn't heard from him. But it was a good thing he hadn't read it. With its new *grab 'em* opening, it was much more likely to get him excited now. He'd read it in one sitting and be on the phone immediately organising a lunch so that he could put forward his sales strategy. Milly smiled ruefully. In the four mostly painful years that he'd represented her, she had met him only twice and spoken to him possibly six times. Still, she could live in hope.

CHAPTER THREE

Jonson felt proud of himself as he went into Heathrow with his fellow business travellers. His christening injuries had turned out to be a blessing. Unable to wear a helmet over his bandages, he'd expected to be laid up and skint for at least a month, but he had been assigned to the personal courier division. He hadn't even known it existed, but was glad that it did. Now he had to deliver important packages in person. He'd spent three weeks accompanying packages to Edinburgh, Birmingham and Glasgow, but today his destination was New York.

Report to the British Airways ticket desk with pass- port, pick up tickets. Depart 10.25 a.m., arrive New York 12.25 local time. You will be met at the airport by a car and taken to Crédit Suisse First Boston at 1664 Madison Avenue, to leave package serial number TSH03 with a Mr Lance Craddock, Snr Vice-President, Marketing. Depart New York . . .

He felt like an athlete as he bounded down the travelator at what seemed like superhuman speed and he literally flew into Terminal Four, the glamour terminal, where the jumbos hung out, ready for their long-haul flights. He'd stayed at Milly's place last night because it was convenient for the airport, and she'd explained how he could try to get himself upgraded to business class, but he wasn't bothered. He was flying *on business* and that was all that mattered. The size of his seat and how far it reclined were irrelevant. As long as he had a seat and an overhead locker for his baggage, he was okay. And he was only taking hand luggage with him on a three-thousand-mile flight! How cool was that?

The British Airways ticket desk wasn't busy and Jonson was at the head of the queue. An attractive girl was serving an elderly gentleman, and Jonson hoped that she'd be done before her two male colleagues so that she could attend to him. He smiled as he noted the old man bend down to retrieve his bag. No doubt she'd speeded up having seen the prize that was on offer next. She needn't have bothered with her flashing light. As the old man peeled away, a beaming Jonson was upon her.

'Hi there,' he said, with the bizarre North American twang that he noticed Pierce Brosnan had on *Parkinson* the other evening. 'Jonson Clarke flying to New York . . . and coming back today,' he added nonchalantly, as if it were no big deal.

There wasn't even a flicker of admiration in her face – he might as well have asked for a London Underground Travel Card. On reflection, he decided she wasn't so attractive after all. He'd just been caught up in the airport thing – there was something about women who worked for airlines . . . the uniforms, the tans, the manicured hands, the hair tied up, the hats. Basically, they always looked groomed and up for it. This one didn't seem up for anything.

Ticket in hand, he set off for the check-in desks with a

banking document worth millions of dollars and another of less value but infinitely more importance.

'I'm taking your script with me,' he had said to Milly last night.

'It's no good just taking it with you.'

'I know. I'm going to read it too.'

Milly didn't look convinced. 'There and back, Jonson. That gives you at least sixteen hours.'

'I'm gonna read it. I promise.'

'Well, good. I hope you enjoy it. You should do – it's about you, after all.'

Jonson felt terrible that he hadn't already read it. It was nearly a month since his christening débâcle and he'd had a copy for all that time. Georgina hadn't helped either. She'd turned the wretched thing round in one day. He knew how important the script was to Milly, and now he was determined not to let her down.

Eight o'clock in the morning was a punishing time for a meeting with Mr Mahmood, pontificating about the wonders of hotels.

'I have discovered a problem with toilett waste,' he announced with his finger held in the air. He paused for dramatic effect but it didn't work. No one really understood what he meant.

'Does anyboddy know whatt thatt problem might be?'

Milly hoped that it might be the hundreds of individually laundered hand towels that the washrooms so wastefully got through each day.

'For some reason,' he continued, 'we are having solidds that are avoiding the flush.'

34

If Milly hadn't known the man she would have laughed, or thought it was a joke, but she knew it wasn't and she rolled her eyes. Surely she was destined to participate in meetings worthier than these. Other people in the room less experienced than her were still confused, and it took Lucas to clarify the situation.

'You mean floaters, sir.'

Mr Mahmood glared at him. Clearly he considered these 'floaters' as a serious threat to the hotel's five-star status.

'Do you know what it iss that the guests first do when they gett into their roomms?'

'Put on the TV, sir,' Carlos offered. He was a particularly irksome graduate with a reputation to forge, and had yet to learn that Mr Mahmood loved his rhetorical questions.

'No, Carlos. Not the teevee,' he snapped. 'Our data shows that the teevee is seconnde.' He had a wealth of spurious research data to corroborate every point he ever made. 'The first thing a guest does in the roome is check out the bathroome, so just thinke about that for a seconnd eh. They checkk into their roome, whatt is the firsst thing they will see?' He raised his hand, so that everyone knew it was a question he was about to answer himself. 'They'rre going to see someone else's sheete.' Milly closed her eyes slowly.

Everyone was asked to be vigilant and to check toilets discreetly whenever they could. It was ludicrous but typical of the man and, for Milly, it was all thoroughly depressing. An intelligent and attractive young woman on the lookout for buoyant faeces. It was even more alarming to her that her only planned escape route from this ordeal was to become a film-maker, no less, and that was seeming increasingly unlikely. She still hadn't heard from Lyal, although she hadn't really expected to. Today however, she would start chasing him for a response, albeit politely of course.

Jonson made his way haughtily through the airport, his leather soles making hard work of the highly polished floor. With his bandaged head and suit, he looked distinctly odd, like a cultural attaché from a very remote country indeed. The last time he'd worn his suit his head had caught fire, but he couldn't afford to be superstitious. He was flying to New York on business, albeit in economy, and therefore he needed to dress like a businessman.

The airport was busy with people buying books and magazines, toiletries and booze, and, as usual, there was an array of beautiful women for Jonson to gawp at. Beautiful women from all four corners of the world; expert, no doubt, in the universal language of sex. He'd always found airports exciting, sexy places, and today, coupled with the prospect of his first business flight, his hormones were raging.

There were countless check-in desks dealing with flights that spanned the globe. To be sure of getting his seat, Jonson had arrived at the airport three hours ahead of the scheduled departure time so there was no queue for his flight. A few desks down, there was a long meandering queue of jogging trousers and football shirts destined for Orlando. Pasty-faced people desperate to get sun-burnt.

'Hello, sir. Could I have your passport and ticket,

please?' said the polite black British Airways clerk. Jonson liked him immediately and handed them over. 'Any baggage, sir?'

It was the question he'd been looking forward to all morning, and he cherished his one-word answer. It was a truly great moment for him and, if he wasn't mistaken, the dude working for BA seemed to share it with him.

'One moment, Mr Clarke. I need to make a quick telephone call to the desk.'

Jonson couldn't recall the last time he'd been called Mr Clarke. The clerk read Jonson's details into the phone. Then his attention was inevitably drawn to his passenger's cranium. Jonson smiled as the man dropped his eyes awkwardly. He deserved to know: he was a brother and one that had given up respect for his hand-luggage-only status.

'Caught fire,' Jonson volunteered.

The clerk winced. 'Ah, man.'

'Yeah, man. Whole thing went up.'

'Must have hurt.'

'Yeah, kinda,' he said casually deciding to skip the fact that it was actually more embarrasing than painful. 'Had a big Afro, didn't I? Puff.' Jonson blew his cheeks out and used his hands to demonstrate the explosion.

The clerk was obviously desperate to ask how, but he was too polite. He was a British Airways employee, after all.

'I'm a stuntman,' Jonson said. He hadn't intended to lie but it had just popped out. Actually, he was quite pleased with it. He liked the idea of being a stuntman. 'I'm a stunt double in movies,' he added.

'Safe, man. Which movie?' The BA-speak had now been replaced by street.

'I was working on the recent Bond film.'

'Straight up?'

'Yeah, man. I'm a stunt double for Brosnan. Got too close to a burning oil rig. I just lit up.'

'*You're a stunt double for Brosnan?*' The clerk was incredulous.

How indeed could a black dude with an Afro double for a white guy? By now Jonson had realised his folly and was searching for an appropriate explanation.

'It was a night scene.'

'What?'

Luckily, the person at the other end of the phone line distracted the check-in official. He put down the phone, and looked up suspiciously at the stuntman.

'Mr Clarke, your flight today is actually fully booked and . . .'

Jonson's heart sank. Things had been going too well. I should have known, he thought.

'. . . and because it's full we'd like to upgrade you to the business cabin. If that's okay with you, of course.'

'Business class?' Jonson pointed to himself in disbelief.

'If that's okay with you. You don't have—'

'No. It's fine.'

It always irked Jonson when every player interviewed clutching a winner's medal at Wembley said it hadn't sunk in yet, but now he understood exactly what they meant. Jonson didn't need to answer. His display of beaming white teeth said it all.

*   *   *

When the Shelton Tower, Park Lane, was busy, its problem with staff shortages became apparent. The hotel industry relies heavily on foreign labour because it's dirt cheap and isn't likely to walk out if it doesn't get its statutory number of breaks. In fact, the best employees, from a hotel's perspective, are illegal immigrants because they can be officially exploited: officially they don't exist.

Reception was busy. Umpteen manicured fingers were drumming on the white marble desk as their owners waited impatiently to be served by an increasingly frantic Milly and her team. To be busy and short staffed compromised them. Their inclination was to speed up check-in, which meant dispensing with the five-star service: *'Here you go. Room 468. Lift's over there, fourth floor. Follow the numbers round. Okay, next!'* This wouldn't do at the Shelton Tower, Park Lane, not under the stewardship of Mr Mahmood.

Milly, ever the professional, looked up from her monitor and smiled. 'There we are, Mr Ridgeon. You're in Room 568 on the fifth floor. The lifts are through the atrium to your left and your room is on the right as you exit the lift. Your luggage will be brought to your room. I do hope you enjoy your stay.' Do remember to flush your toilet twice please, she would have loved to have added.

'Sorry about that, Mr Donovan, your account is just being printed now,' Milly said, scurrying back to him. Mr Samuel Donovan III, president of the Beattie Corporation Inc., looked at her fleetingly. He wasn't accustomed to being kept waiting.

Out of the corner of her eye, Milly could see that Mr

Donovan was admiring himself in the Gothic mirror hanging behind her. Satisfied that he was looking suitably presidential, he fixed his gaze on Milly. She was well used to the attentions of the guests. It was no secret that Mr Mahmood only staffed his reception with his most attractive female employees and he'd made Milly his team captain for this very reason. Her beauty was natural and understated. Her clear unblemished skin made her appear younger than she was, and her thick shining black hair and bright green eyes gave away her Irish ancestry. Georgina complained bitterly about women like her, the 'blessed people' as she described them. Milly could feel the eyes of President Donovan roving up and down her torso, wondering whether she had the bottom half to match the top.

On her screen, she noticed that President Donovan had enjoyed two films during his visit: *Night Pursuits* and *Lusting Playmates*. The sales of in-room adult films were very profitable and had recently exploded. Originally guests had been reluctant to purchase such films. It would have been embarrassing if a female receptionist knew that they'd chosen *Office Frolics* over *Forrest Gump*. The wording in the film guide was changed to read 'All films will appear as FILM on your invoice' and the floodgates were opened. Milly loved the fact that her screen still revealed the truth.

'There we are, Mr Donovan. If you'd just like to—'

His ruby-coloured credit card hit the desk before she could finish. Clearly he didn't need to check his account, but then no self-respecting corporate big hitter ever did. To do so would imply that there were financial limits – guests of the Shelton Tower, Park Lane, didn't have limits.

'Did you enjoy your stay last night?' she asked politely.

'Great.'

I bet you did.

Mr Donovan signed his credit card slip, nodded at Milly and turned to meet his driver, who'd probably stayed at a Travelodge somewhere.

A few heads turned towards Jonson as he eased himself into the business lounge. He was grateful that he'd thought to buy himself a copy of the *Financial Times* – it stopped everyone thinking he was either a boxer or a singer. The lounge was very civilised: PCs with Internet access were available, as were personal stereos and an array of magazines and newspapers. The front cover of *Maxim* featured a blonde girl who defied belief. Jonson dearly wanted to pick it up, but felt it might blow his cover. He poured himself a cup of coffee from the percolator, hoping people would notice that he didn't add any milk or sugar, picked up a copy of the *Economist* and made his way to an empty armchair .

He sipped his acrid coffee and set about the *FT*. His resolve to read it crumbled almost immediately. The front page offered him little. Apparently, the Central European Bank was demanding *tighter fiscal policy* and featured the face of some glum-looking bloke. The sports pages were of little comfort either, only two pages that gave undue coverage to some bloody sailing race.

*   *   *

Albert T. Willenheim was also waiting for the New York flight. He was furious that the first-class cabin was full and that he had to suffer the indignity of a business-class seat. He was barking into his mobile phone: 'Yeah. Well, lady, you tell him it's me on the phone, and I expect he'll wanna cut his meeting short . . . I don't care if she's new. And I don't care for being on hold . . .'

The whole lounge could hear his rant but he didn't care a jot.

Jonson decided that the rude fat guy across the room who was yelling into his phone and sweating like a pig must be a big hitter, most likely the president of Ford cars. His bulbous nose glowed red and his eyes were barely visible below two of the biggest eyebrows Jonson had ever seen. He glanced up at the screen. His flight was boarding in fifteen minutes. It was going to be great. He couldn't wait.

After the morning chaos there was a brief respite at the Shelton Tower. No 'floaters' had been reported and Reception was quiet. Naisi, a trainee from Brazil, was shadowing Lucas for the day. She was young and attractive, and he was keen that she should stay as close to him as possible. Brazilians, like the Swedes, have a generic sexual chemistry. He was disappointed when Naisi explained that she hadn't taken part in any carnivals, but that didn't stop him imagining her in a glittering G-string with a diamond in her navel, cavorting through the streets of Rio.

Milly had skulked into the back office and had her

mobile phone pressed to her ear. Her pursuit of Lyal had begun. He'd had the new script for long enough. It was now game on. 'Hello, Muriel, it's Juliet.'

'Hi, how are you?'

'I don't suppose Lyal's there?'

'He's in a meeting. Could I take a message?'

Milly huffed into the phone, which was about as militant as she got. She was so unlucky. Every time she thought to ring Lyal, he was either on the phone or in a meeting. Milly imagined he must have league tables for his clients. From the 'always get through' league down. Until recently Milly had been in the 'pause' league, where Muriel would check to see whether Lyal would take her call or not. He never did, and it appeared that she'd been recently relegated farther to the 'permanently unavailable' league. The last time she'd called him was to ensure that he didn't read the old version of the script. In effect she was asking Lyal to disregard a script he was already disregarding. She could sense that Muriel felt sorry for her but she didn't want sympathy: she wanted to be treated professionally. 'I don't suppose you know if he's had a chance to look at the script yet?'

'I don't, but I'll certainly pass your message on.'

Muriel had long stopped saying 'Shall I get him to call you?' because even she couldn't be bothered with the pretence any more.

Milly put her phone into her bag angrily, and reappeared in Reception just as the little tornado blew in. Milly knew she was always a reassuring sight for Mr Mahmood.

'Mill-ee,' he said, 'this morning, you were magnificent.

Wee had a lot to deal with, but wee managed. And your calm under the fire was duly noted.'

'Thank you, Mr Mahmood.'

There couldn't be many jobs today in which a university graduate was reduced to calling her boss 'Mr'. He'd never insisted on it and there was nothing to stop her calling him Muhammad, but no one had chanced it.

'Mill-ee, I've bin watching you . . .' Mr Mahmood whispered. Milly shuddered.

An amorous advance from Mr Mahmood was the last thing she needed. 'You watch everyone,' she said.

'Not like I watch you.'

'Really?'

'I've always liked you, Mill-ee . . .'

Milly was now panicking and frantically searching for a reason to knock him back and at that moment was more than happy to announce to the world that she was gay. News that would no doubt send Lucas into a wanking frenzy.

'. . . and this might come as a shock to you but I think you have true managementt potential . . . Yes. I mean it. Real managementt.'

Milly was so relieved that she looked shocked, which Mr Mahmood must have interpreted as joy. 'Oh, yes, Mill-ee.' He pointed upward, indicating just how high she could go. 'Five, ten years' time, you could be doing my job,' he said, and moved off to terrorise someone else, leaving her to reflect on his prediction. The very idea that she might still be at the hotel in ten or even five years' time was harrowing.

*   *   *

44

Jonson made his way down the corridor towards the plane for his first long-haul flight, his first business flight and his first flight on a jumbo. A Chinese or Filipina girl in uniform greeted him on the plane. Must be a perk of business class, he thought, that we get all the fit hostesses.

There was only one available seat left, which was his, of course – next to the lounge fat guy . . .

Willenheim's mood didn't lighten when he saw the bandaged black man approaching with a determined look on his face that they were about to become friends.

'Hello, I'm Jonson Clarke. Going to New York!' the man said, and offered his hand.

Willenheim was dumbfounded. In all his years of flying, people had occasionally introduced themselves, but never so formally, never straight away, and only the captain had ever felt the need to tell him where the plane was heading. It was a seven-hour trip, and Willenheim decided that this situation had to be nipped in the bud. 'I don't talk on planes, son, so don't be getting your life story ready.' He nodded to a pile of scripts he had to read.

'No problem,' Jonson said. He sat down and fiddled with his stereo.

'I also have a lot of work to do. So I expect you won't be playing your music too loudly.'

'You won't hear a thing. I'm heading back to London from New York tonight, so I'll probably want to get some shut-eye myself.'

The strange 'Brosnanesque' accent had returned, and Jonson had no idea where the word 'shut-eye' had come from, but it seemed to work. The American didn't smile, but his face definitely lightened a little. The sides of his mouth at least cracked from their rigid grimace, giving Jonson enough confidence to try again.

'Jonson Clarke. Pleased to meet you,' he said, holding out his hand once more.

This time Willenheim took it.

CHAPTER FOUR

Jonson watched the safety drill only because he felt sorry for the hostess whom everyone else was ignoring. Clearly, they were all frequent travellers, and knew what they should do if the plane landed in the Atlantic. He had fully intended to read Milly's script on the flight but he hadn't bargained on having his own personal television screen and fourteen movies to choose from. He pulled it out of his bag, flicked through the tight text, and groaned. He'd read it on the return flight.

Another stewardess appeared with a tray of champagne flutes, and she enjoyed everyone's individual attention. The intercom hissed, and the rich, smooth, golden voice of the captain filled the cabin: 'Good afternoon, ladies and gentlemen. My name is Captain Bridge, and I'd like to welcome you aboard this Boeing 747 this morning for our flight to New York . . . My apologies for our delay since you boarded the aircraft this morning, there's been a little air-traffic congestion, but that seems to have sorted itself out now, and we should be away very shortly. I do trust that our cabin staff have been looking after you during this delay . . .'

Jonson brought his chair up from an almost horizontal position and had his face pressed up against his window ready for take-off. The huge bird had finished its taxi and was about to plunge itself down the runway.

'Cabin crew. Spot checks and seats, please.'

'Missssster Clarrke.'

It wasn't a good time to disturb him. What could they possibly want? He had his seat belt on, his chair was upright and his footrest was tucked away. He turned round angrily.

The hostess who'd welcomed him on to the plane was smiling at him, holding a tray of empty champagne flutes. Jonson added his to the tray. She noted that he hadn't yet finished his luxury nut selection.

'Misssster Clarrke. Would you like me to hold your nuts for take-off?'

Jonson smiled before looking over at Willenheim and winking.

'Eh . . . Now that's what I call a bloody upgrade.'

Milly's mobile phone chirped at her. It was highly unlikely, but maybe Lyal was returning her call, she thought. She scrambled through her bag and grabbed it.

'Hello?'

'It's me.'

Milly's heart sank. Lyal wasn't a woman. 'Hi, George.'

'Oh. Sorr*ee*!'

'Me too. Just thought it might have been Lyal, that's all.'

'We're on for tonight, I take it?'

Georgina sounded curt and matter-of-fact, which irritated Milly. 'Yes, why wouldn't I be?'

Lucas popped his head into the office and made it

obvious he wanted to interrupt. 'Hang on, George,' she said, then nodded to Lucas to speak.

'Erm, Georgina wants you to call her.' He was gone by the time the information registered, and Milly made a mental note to bollock him later.

'I hear you've called today already,' she said to her friend in a conciliatory tone.

'Three bloody times.'

'Lucas has only just told me.'

'He wants sacking. How can you work on a reception desk and not give someone messages? Anyway, see you tonight at seven thirty. My place.'

'His name?' Milly rolled her eyes.

'Whose name?'

'*His* name. I take it it's a bloke you're lining me up for.'

'Oh blimey, sorry Milly. Erm. Hang on. Alex. Yep that's it.'

Milly hung up feeling depressed. It seemed Georgina had been consulting a list. Full of eligible bachelors happy to spend an evening having Marks and Spencer warm-ups and a not-quite-defrosted cheesecake. She hoped she might be near the end of the list, but feared she was probably still only on the As.

Tonight would be the fifth dinner party Georgina had thrown to end Milly's single status, a status she was more than happy with but unable to convince Georgina on. None of the introductions had led to anything so far, and Milly didn't hold out any hope for this one, although Georgina had assured her that tonight's contestant was a highly desirable recent divorcé. Early viewing was essential to avoid disappointment. Milly would have been a less reluctant guest if Georgina hadn't been so blatant and crude about the whole charade. Perhaps invite over a whole bunch of people to relieve the pressure somewhat; hold an informal drinks-and-nibbles do, allowing our heroine to mingle, just like at a buffet, choosing what she likes and avoiding what she doesn't. But no, Georgina preferred a more up close and personal touch, which was usually excruciatingly embarrassing. It would be just the four of them: the happily married Georgina and David, Milly and some poor sod from David's office commandeered for the evening by David's wife.

Willenheim was returning to his seat from the toilet. He looked troubled, as if he'd just found a lump in his scrotum. In Hollywood, 'job security' is associated with dentists, personal trainers and plastic surgeons, not studio bosses. Not even stars are immune. How would Burt Reynolds in his heyday have taken the news that by the nineties he'd be starring in a Specsavers commercial with a bloke who was famous for getting sunburnt? Pacific Studios hadn't had a box-office bonanza under Willenheim's reign, and the current crop of movies about to be released didn't augur well.

Willenheim was feeling the heat. His remit was to put bums on cinema seats, and that meant producing movies that people wanted to see. The purpose of his latest European jaunt was to meet the various film luminaries who'd been working on scripts with Mitch Carmichael.

When he got back to his seat, he was happy to see that his neighbour was still engrossed in the moronic *Ice Heroes*, one of Pacific's recent efforts. It had performed badly Stateside but maybe it would get lucky in Europe. Taking solace from Jonson enjoying his movie was categorical proof that he was indeed a worried man. It was as if Jonson sensed the role he had to play. With his ever unfortunate timing, he took off his headphones. 'That *Ice Heroes* was SHIT!'

Willenheim was suddenly more miserable than he'd ever imagined it was possible to be. But his spirits were about to plummet twenty thousand feet lower.

'But this is great.' Jonson pointed at the screen, and roared with laughter. Willenheim glanced at the picture. *New York Winters*. He'd turned it down in favour of the bombed *Ice Heroes*. To distract himself from the panic that had now assailed him, he opened a script, *The Honorary Consulate*, by Sebastian Cartwright. Mitch had summarised it for him: 'A nineteenth-century tale of intrigue and romance between an American consul and the heir to the British throne.' He began reluctantly to read, got halfway through page one and stopped.

Willenheim shut the script, closed his eyes and breathed out heavily. What was wrong with these people? What was wrong with *rich man is lost, asks directions from beautiful prostitute. They fall in love and have great fun along the way?*

Mitch Carmichael was thirty-five, and beginning to look older. The stress was showing, and no amount of exercise and moisturiser could help. He'd been in the business since he was five, a child star. He was never as big as Jodie Foster, but all child actors are called stars. Then he had moppish blond hair, large blue eyes and a cute little nose.

He'd been spotted by a neighbour who was a commercials casting director and, after two successful Kellogg's campaigns, had been cast in a long-running western drama called *Madison Mountain*. It was a poor relation to *The Little House on the Prairie* but it kept Mitch employed for six years. Sadly it was to be his acting zenith: adolescence was cruel to him and his good looks didn't return until he was into his late teens. By then his acting days were over. But he was bright enough to maintain the contacts he had made on *Madison* and had settled down to develop a career in movie development.

In the film industry, nepotism and luck play crucial roles in equal measure. Mitch had no famous forebears to haul him up the slippery pole, but he encountered his fair share of good fortune. And, uniquely in ego-fuelled Hollywood, he had the humility to appreciate it. When he was thirty he became head of Development at Fox after five years' steady success at Paramount. Careers can be made on the strength of one hit movie and Mitch's was *Dinner Parties*, one of four low-budget movies he supervised in his first year at Fox. It wasn't very good and no one had expected it to do well, but it attracted a cult following among college students, and eventually it was showing in all the US art cinemas and providing a lucrative return for the studio. Mitch was hailed as a Development genius – and had been trying ever since to live up to his reputation. Fêted by all the major studios, he eventually plumped for Pacific, after they made him an irresistible financial offer. It was a coup for both parties, but Pacific expected much of him, and the pressure increased daily. Mr Willenheim wanted dollar results and it was Mitch's job to provide them.

And it followed that if Willenheim, the studio boss, was suffering, then all those directly below him should suffer too. As head of Development, this was especially true for Mitch. *Ice Heroes* had been his baby and, before that, he'd presided over *Blind Romance*, another whopping self-basting turkey. It was a double blow for Mitch. Its opening weekend was catastrophic and after two ruinous weeks it was pulled. The studio's big summer movie had crashed and so had Mitch's marriage to its star. She left him for the male lead.

Pacific Studios occupied a beautiful art-deco building in Los Angeles. It was white, with pastel-coloured trims that ran down the sides to its magnificent central entrance. Even the carpark was glamorous, filled with beautiful, mostly European cars.

This morning the sun was pouring in through the windows, but none of the occupants of Meeting Room Two had noticed. Mitch was chairing a meeting of his team ahead of Willenheim's arrival.

The speakerphone bleeped, and Dolores' mechanical voice sent a shiver through the room: 'Mr Willenheim is arriving at Newark in four hours, and being met by the studio jet. You should expect a meeting with him today at whatever time he arrives. I'm speaking with him in half an hour. Any questions?'

'No. Thank you, Dolores. We're all looking forward to seeing him,' Mitch said.

'Yeah, right.' Dolores hung up.

Mitch thought about turning off the machine. But

before he could Dolores was back. 'I've just had last month's sales figures through, Mitch. You might want to take a look at them ahead of your showdown this evening.'

'She did say showdown, didn't she?' he asked his team.

They nodded, and each seemed relieved that they weren't him. It was his ass on the line, not theirs. His demise would be sad because everyone liked him, but it would also present one of them with a foothold on the greasy pole. Those in show business, as in no other, celebrate another person's failure as a victory of their own. When *Waterworld* showed signs that it was leaking, it must have felt like a special ray of sunshine on the patios of A-list stars, and after its opening weekend the Malibu skyline was no doubt blotted out by the fumes from celebratory barbecues.

Mitch gathered himself together and rubbed his hands. 'So, Willenheim's back tonight, and hopefully he'll have read the six scripts we've all been working on.'

'I don't reckon he will,' Josie said.

'Me neither.' Scott added.

'I got a call last night from Ryan. He said that Willenheim would *definitely* have read the scripts,' Claudia said firmly.

Mitch didn't like Claudia. She was new to his department, and clearly had designs on his job. She was young, maybe twenty-five, boringly attractive, and terrifyingly ambitious. Mitch didn't care for the way she had just quoted Ryan. Why had he spoken with her? And, more to the point, why was he still in Europe with Willenheim and not Mitch? It was a clear challenge to Mitch's authority: he could bawl her out, or he could pretend to be so secure in his job that he hadn't noticed her challenge.

'Thank you for that, Claudia.' He'd wimped out. 'Anything else we should know about?' he asked.

Claudia shook her head, having enjoyed her little victory.

'Well, I hope he *has* read them, because I think they're all damn fine scripts and any of them would make a worthy picture for this studio. By this evening, I'm hoping to have at least one green light, possibly two.'

'Which ones, Mitch?' Scott asked, apparently trying to restore his boss's credibility.

'Well, we've all got our favourites, but I'm hoping *The Honorary Consulate* gets the go-ahead. It's exactly what the market wants.' He said with as much conviction as an ex-child star could muster.

With no time to go home and change, Milly headed straight from work for the dinner party *chez* nightmare.

She arrived at Georgina's door and knocked. She felt like a winning contestant on *Blind Date* just before the screen is pulled back. She didn't have to wait long as she could hear Georgina's footsteps urgently pounding down the stairs of their exorbitantly overpriced townhouse. The door flew open, and a frantic-looking Georgina pulled her inside. She looked hassled, as if she had something to explain, but before she could a voice behind her said, 'Hello, you must be Milly.' An elderly man had come into the hallway from the sitting room.

Milly stared at him, speechless.

'Milly, can I introduce Alex?'

Dumbfounded, Milly held out her hand.

'Oh, please, call me Al,' said the man. He took her hand and kissed it.

Alex was older than her dad, Milly thought. No, he was older than her granddad had been when he died. Alex had once been handsome, she could see. Now, though, with his Blake Carrington silver mane, he was well into his distinguished phase.

'You're even more beautiful than Georgina said,' he stated, looking her up and down slowly. He was still holding her hand. Milly shot a glance at Georgina, who returned one of her own. He's loaded, it said. But Milly had never understood the allure of money. Of course, nice things were important to her. She would love her bath-room to be wall-to-wall Chanel, but she couldn't conceive of waking up next to Michael Winner to get it.

Alex was exactly like a guest at the Shelton Tower, Park Lane, and it was quite liberating for Milly to meet his type out of work because she didn't have to stroke his ego. It annoyed her that he appeared so relaxed about the disparity between their ages. Like she was actually looking for a husband who would need helping out of the bath in five years' time.

'Georgina tells me you've written a brilliant screen-play,' he remarked.

'Actually, we're looking for finance now. You haven't got five million quid handy, have you?'

Alex laughed far too hard and loudly. When he had finished, Milly continued, 'So, have you?'

'Well, it's funny you should say that,' he began, 'because some chums of mine in the City are cash rich and they're looking . . .'

Milly had gathered enough experience of the film industry to understand that this was hot air, and she tuned herself out of the conversation altogether.

The meal was torturous. Alex had the skin of a rhino and didn't seem concerned when Milly established that she was younger than any of his four children from his two marriages. He was the senior partner in David's company, and bored her rigid with tales of his business exploits throughout the world. The only way she'd be seeing him again was if he honoured his promise to give the Shelton Tower his firm's account for visiting clients. Mr Mahmood would weep tears of ecstasy when she told him. Which, of course, she would do. Such a demonstration of her commitment to the hotel was worth at least a Saturday off.

'Coffee, anyone?' Georgina asked.

'Yes, please,' Alex said, and Milly saw an opportunity to finally end her misery.

'Er, no thanks, George, I've got to get going. Early start in the morning.'

'I'll run you home,' Alex said, quick as a flash.

'Don't be silly, Alex. You haven't had your coffee yet.'

'We can have some at yours. I insist.'

I bet you do, Grandpa. She didn't want to be rude because he was David's boss, but he did need the door slamming in his face.

'Actually, I've got my car,' she lied. 'But it was nice meeting you—'

'I'll be in touch,' Alex interrupted.

Georgina had got up from the table as well as a way of ensuring her friend's escape. Milly made a point of giving David a kiss on the lips accompanied by a loving hug, and then turned to Alex, who was girding himself for a bit of the same and was disappointed by a formal handshake.

'And I'll have a word with my chums in the City about your film,' he said, sounding hopeful.

Milly didn't fall for it: Alex had more chance of getting her into bed than he did of getting her film off the ground. 'That'd be great,' she said. She was desperate for a break, but not so desperate as to be stupid.

As soon as they couldn't be heard, Georgina immediately began to apologise.

'No more dates, George.'

'Absolutely. I don't know what David was thinking.'

'He wasn't. At least not about me anyway.'

Georgina was hurt by the implication and Milly immediately regretted it. 'Sorry. I didn't mean that. I shouldn't be mad at David, when it was so clearly your doing.'

'Guilty as charged. Sorry.'

'Accepted.'

'Hang on, I'll get the car keys. I take it the car thing was a lie.'

Milly smiled. Georgina returned with a mischievous look on her face. 'Here, this'll make it up to you.' She tossed a set of car keys at Milly, and she immediately noticed the smart leather Porsche tag.

'I'm not taking David's, I couldn't.'

''Course you can. It's only a bloody car, although to hear him go on about it . . . I keep telling him, I don't care how many horses it represents.'

'But he'll go mad.'

'I won't tell him. I'll let him think it's been nicked. Keep him going right up until he's about to push the final nine.' Milly sniggered at the imagery.

'Just make sure you don't crash it, or we'll both be single.'

'Tempting,' Milly said as they hugged each other goodbye.

The lights in the cabin were dimmed, and most of the occupants were asleep. Willenheim had been ploughing through the scripts but was taking a five-minute break to talk to Ryan, whom he'd called up from luggage class.

'*Honorary Consulate*, my ass. Do you think American kids give a shit about what happened to some fag from France over two hundred years ago?'

'Absolutely not,' Ryan said. As a vice-president of the finance division, he had nothing to gain from hammering another nail into Mitch's coffin, but he did it anyway.

'I need scripts with warmth,' Willenheim went on, to a succession of nods from Ryan. 'Scripts with real characters having a great time, getting something done. Jesus, why can't people write stories any more? Is it so fucking hard?'

'It shouldn't be,' Ryan offered.

'Well, why don't you write one, then?' Willenheim snarled. '*It's a Wonderful Life* right through to *Working Girl* – great fucking stories, and that's what I asked for.

So what do I get? Some crock of shit about men in tights.'

It was typical of Jonson that he should have on his lap exactly what Willenheim needed, but he couldn't hear a word the man was saying, busy as he was with his head-phones clamped to his head, listening to Kool and the Gang.

CHAPTER FIVE

Mitch and his team finally left the office at eight o'clock when Dolores called to say that the meeting was postponed until tomorrow morning first thing. What did that mean? What time was *first thing*? Seven, eight, nine – six o'clock, even. He decided that the ambiguity was deliberate but, for sure, he wasn't going to miss that meeting. No one kept Willenheim waiting, and Mitch deduced that his boss was counting on him not being there so he could fire his ass.

This, of course, was ridiculous. Willenheim didn't need to dress up a case for firing an employee. The case could be as simple as: *You've got a moustache and your name is not Tom Selleck*. The only thing he hated more than men with moustaches was women with moustaches, and over the years he had dispatched many a hairy executive into the 'available for hire' Hollywood executive slush pool. Firings were a perk of a studio boss's job. They imbued him with power, authority and status, which increased in relation to the pettiness of the sackee's offence, and how resolutely they were dealt with.

Mitch had never seen Willenheim in the office before 8.30, and concluded that eight would be a safe time for his team to reconvene. It was only later that night, when he couldn't sleep, that he remembered he was being set up. He'd be in by seven. He'd spent his evening familiarising himself with his development notes on the six scripts. He needed to be prepared for whatever objections Willenheim put up. At least he'd done his job – it wasn't his fault that America's writers were turning in crap.

If the bouquet of flowers from Alex had been delivered to her home, they would have looked amazing, but against the tropical jungle of the Shelton Tower they looked more like a garage forecourt special offer. The message made her toes curl: *Last night, the pleasure was all mine.* You're telling me, mate, she thought, as she threw it into the bin. Irritatingly, Lucas speedily retrieved it.

'It was nothing exciting, Lucas. Just a dinner party. That's what adults do, you know.'

'Come off it, Milly. *"The pleasure was all mine"* . . . blowjob, eh?'

Milly would have laughed but for the fact that the idea of such an act with someone as wrinkly as Alex made her feel ill.

Today's excitement was the arrival of Venom, the rock band. Except no one at the hotel, other than Mr Mahmood, had ever heard of them. Apparently they'd been massive in the seventies and had recently re-formed, no doubt having run out of money. Mr Mahmood stopped mentioning any more of their colossal hits once he realised that he was still on his own. He also declined Lucas's suggestion that he should thrash one of them out. He had last seen them at Phoenix University in 1972. No one had ever considered him as a possible rock fan, and

Milly couldn't imagine him fitting in at a Venom concert – the only fan in ironed clothes with a short-back-and-sides.

'A real rock-and-roll band for a change. Not like the rabbish we have now,' Mr Mahmood enthused at their morning meeting.

'Mr Mahmood, shouldn't you stay in Reception today?' Milly suggested.

'You thinke?'

'You'll be the only person who'll recognise them. And you know how it is when celebs don't get recognised.'

'Don't worry. You'll recognise them when you see them.'

'What should we be looking out for?'

'Receding ponytails and cap-sleeve T-shirts, I reckon,' Lucas chimed in, with which Mr Mahmood agreed, although he didn't understand why everyone else should find this funny.

'Venom. Fancy calling yourself Venom,' Milly scoffed to Lucas.

'Totally clichéd. Especially after Whitesnake,' Lucas agreed.

Milly laughed. 'Whitesnake. God, yeah. Well, at least I've heard of them.'

'My dad went to school with their drummer, you know.'

'What, in America?'

'No. Dorset. I think they're all from round there.'

'Whitesnake are English?' Milly exclaimed. 'But they sound so American.'

'Yeah. That's the idea. The American rock sound.'

Milly laughed. 'Yeah. Via Poole. Whitesnake are English! Surely if they're English, they should be Grass Snake,' she suggested, using her hands to better visualise the name in lights. 'Or Wasp Sting,' she added.

Lucas chortled. 'No, no, I've got it. Playing live tonight, all the way from Tiverton, in Devon, p-l-ease welcome on to the stage – Stinging Nettle.'

Mitch lay in his bed waiting for his alarm to indicate that his miserable night was over. As far as he could tell, he hadn't slept at all. At 6 a.m. it sprang into life, but Mitch was already in his *en suite* bathroom shaving.

His clothes from the previous day were hanging on the exercise bike that his wife hadn't bothered taking with her because her new beau had his own gym. She had even had the gall to ask him to store it for her until they split up.

Half an hour later, he was turning the corner of Fifth Street, and Pacific Studios loomed impressively large before him. It was another beautiful morning. He pulled the car to a halt at the security cabin and lowered his electric window. 'Morning, Kenny. You look tired, buddy,' he shouted over to the elderly guard, who had probably once been head of development here himself. One turkey too many, and now the highlight of his day was turning away someone without a pass.

'You're early, Mitch.'

Strange how people perpetually pointed out the obvious, Mitch mused.

'You here for that meeting as well?' Kenny asked.

Mitch's smile vanished. Questions flashed through his mind. How did Kenny know about the meeting? And he had said 'as well'. Someone had already arrived. Mitch had a vision of himself by this afternoon being shown which button raised the barrier and which one lowered it.

'Fuck,' he muttered to himself, and he trod on the accelerator and screeched into the compound. Willenheim's Bentley wasn't there but that didn't mean he wasn't in. He often sent his driver off on errands, although that was unlikely at this early hour. There was only one other car in the lot and, worryingly, it wasn't one he recognised. It was a brand-new silver 328i convertible BMW, nicer, newer and sexier than the one Mitch was driving . . .

Mitch pushed open his office door at a few minutes before seven and wasn't surprised at all to be greeted by Claudia. 'Hi, Mitch, how are you doing?' she said, rather awkwardly. 'Thought I'd get in early – catch up on some paperwork.'

Bitch! Mitch had every reason to be paranoid about Claudia. She'd made the same calculations as he had about *first thing* and had hoped to be there ahead of him.

'I wasn't expecting any of the team until eight,' he said, and threw his keys on to the table.

'Like I said, I had a few things I needed to straighten out.'

'Such as?'

'Oh, nothing important, you know . . . the usual stuff.'

'No. I don't. Tell me,' Mitch responded tersely. He regretted backing down from her yesterday, and if indeed this was going to be his last day, it would be a day she wouldn't forget either.

'Well.'

Claudia didn't have an answer for him, and her confidence seemed somewhat dented.

'Nice car you've got yourself,' he said stiffly. Meaning, How the hell does a little girl like you get a car like that?

'It was a graduation present.'

'Really. I take it you came top of the class.'

Claudia glared, and Mitch knew he'd scored a – cheap – point. But he wasn't ashamed. How dare some jumped-up little rich girl join my team and, at the first opportunity, start looking for my fucking job? Hollywood was full of girls like Claudia. Her dad was a well-known Hollywood dentist who counted half of LA's A-list as his clients, including a certain Albert T. Willenheim. No doubt Willenheim's perfectly square teeth had cost him dear, but with Claudia's ambition they looked set to cost Mitch an awful lot more.

Milly didn't notice the odd-looking character enter the hotel, although Samson the doorman did. There was no dress code at the Shelton Tower, but most of its guests wore either suits or designer casuals. This fat balding man wore casuals, but they were not by any designer still in business. He sported cowboy boots and skintight jeans, and a skull-and-crossbones cap-sleeved T-shirt completed the dinosaur look. Although it was overcast and drizzling outside, he wore sunglasses because he didn't want to be recognised. He needn't have worried: apart from his mother, only Mr Mahmood would have realised he was Snake, the lead singer of Venom, and he wasn't in Reception.

Samson had also been looking forward to the arrival of the rock stars. He rated hotel guests by the size of their tips and he was currently mining a rich vein of South Africans, keen to display just how unprejudiced they were when faced with a black man holding a door open for them. He was disappointed that the only thing Snake forced into his hand was his own, before he proceeded to complete a ridiculous handshake, which predictably ended up as a fist.

Milly glanced at the strange-looking collection of men in ill-fitting clothes with paunches who were shambling towards her desk. They had to be Venom. One, a languid-looking individual, stepped up to the desk and gazed at her expectantly.

'Hello, sir. Welcome to the Shelton Tower, Park Lane. You wouldn't happen to be Venom, would you?' Milly said.

The man looked at her with delight stamped across his face. It had been twenty years since their last hit, they were some six thousand miles from home, yet they had been *recognised*. It didn't occur to him that the hotel had been expecting them, and that they couldn't be Nissan's board of directors.

'Yeah, that's right,' he replied.

Venom were in London to do a one-off promotional show for a rock-compilation album, *The Legends of Rock*, that featured one Venom track, which was being released during their tour. It included more notable bands, like Deep Purple, Nirvana and Guns 'N Roses, but most of this talent was either dead or infirm, and only

Venom had been available to appear at the launch in Oxford Street at HMV.

The man with whom Milly was dealing was Stu Summers, the band's manager, whose main function now was to procure the best narcotics that their limited resources could afford. Now he was labouring to fill in the six registration cards, and it was clear that the pass-port numbers would be way beyond him. He pushed them back to her, and as she picked them up she felt a wild desire to laugh. Their names were Snake, Dragon, Devil, Cokey, Headcase and Animal. There were no surnames, but these guys certainly didn't need them with first names like these. Milly excused herself and fled to the back office, where she let rip.

It felt like ages before she had composed herself enough to return to Reception. Fortunately none of them even seemed to have realised that she'd gone, busy as they were trying to work out why there were four clocks on the wall. She allocated them three adjoining rooms on the fourth floor and directed them to the lift.

Venom headed off in the opposite direction from which she'd sent them. She thought of correcting them but then decided not to. They were walking towards Mr Mahmood's office. She hoped they might all meet up again. They deserved each other.

Mitch's team assembled in dribs and drabs, and by 8.15 his mean, lean, fighting development machine was complete and quaking to its very core. It was now 10.30 and Willenheim still hadn't shown. His nerves frayed, Mitch had now turned his conspiracy theory in a different direction: Willenheim wasn't going to show up at all. That was how little he thought of the scripts Mitch had developed. Scott tried to offer words of consolation, but could muster only clichés from the *about-to-be-fired* stockroom: 'Whatever happens today, Mitch, he can't take away your track record. I mean, *Dinner Parties*—'

'Yeah, thanks, Scott.'

Willenheim always liked to make a big entrance, and usually found reason to speak to the office from his car to flag his arrival. Word would spread through the office like Legionnaires' Disease, so that everyone was ready to welcome Caesar. The disadvantage of this strategy was that it took away the element of surprise and meant he couldn't catch people unawares. But it was a minor sacrifice to make in ensuring that the red carpet was rolled out for him.

That morning, when Dolores called to say that the presidential Bentley was on its way, a few sphincters tightened, but none more so than Mitch's. As the car swept majestically into the lot, Mitch watched from his window. The chauffeur leapt out and opened the rear door with a flourish. Willenheim's enormous bulk emerged. Mitch gulped. Maybe Willenheim had a mountain of important things to attend to and had forgotten about him. That would suit him fine – he'd have another twelve months of gainful employment, time in which to find another *Pretty Woman* or *As Good as It Gets*. Mitch watched the big man disappear into the building. He was about to find out just how *first thing* he was.

It wasn't long before his phone bleeped. He picked it up.

Dolores was to the point. 'Could you and your team assemble in the boardroom immediately.' It wasn't a question.

Mitch hung up and swallowed hard. He looked around the anxious faces gathered before him. 'We're on.'

In the boardroom Mitch and his team waited silently for Willenheim and his entourage. They all knew the scripts and had assured Mitch they were right behind him. Of course, he knew they weren't. They *wanted* to be, but that would have been foolhardy. He couldn't blame them – in their position he'd have been the same.

The room was dominated by an enormous mahogany table, and the walls were covered with posters of the studio's great triumphs. That was the pressing problem for Mitch as head of development: all these triumphs were in the past, and he hadn't presided over any of them.

Dolores entered first and took their drinks order. She was closely followed by three suits: Ryan, the snidey little vice-president of Finance, Warren Lassiter, a corporate consultant – whatever the fuck that meant – and Dylan Tizer, head of Legal Affairs and better known as a bondage freak if the rumours were to be believed. With Willenheim's two assistants and Dolores, eleven people were waiting now for the great man. Why so many? The signs weren't good.

Then Willenheim breezed in and everyone started to get up. 'Siddown, siddown. For God's sake,' Willenheim barked.

'Good flight, sir?' Mitch asked, desperate to get off the mark.

'No. Worst fucking flight of my life.'

Mitch tried to look sympathetic.

'First, I'm in club class, and then they sit me next to this moron who irritates the shit out of me for the entire flight. And to top it off there was that crap you'd given me to read.' Willenheim stared directly at Mitch, whose head began to spin and his vision to cloud. Sheer panic began to take its cold grip on him. He felt winded and – although he was sitting with his team, who had to bear equal responsibility for the unfolding calamity – utterly alone. It was as if his team had waited to see how it was going to go, and were now all huddled down at the other end of the table around Willenheim, stroking his hair and feeding him grapes.

'I asked you to develop movies with *warmth*. You remember that?'

'Yes, sir,' Mitch squeaked.

'*The Honorary Consulate* – where's the warmth in that? It's a fucking turkey.'

Mitch felt as if a window had been opened and his team were kindly helping him on to the ledge.

'So, Mitch, imagine the relief I felt when you finally came through.'

The window was suddenly slammed shut as his team hastily shuffled back down to Mitch's end of the table, explaining that they'd been with him all the way.

'A warm, funny story with a happy ending. Makes you laugh and makes you cry . . .'

Willenheim carried on talking as Mitch tried to work out which of the six scripts he was talking about.

'This is a great script,' Willenheim concluded, and held it up.

Mitch was utterly confused. He didn't recognise it because it wasn't bound properly and it didn't even have a Pacific cover.

'*Untitled* by Juliet Millhouse. This is exactly what I've been crying out for.'

'Glad you liked it,' Mitch barely managed. Claudia glared at him.

'You look relieved, Mitch,' Willenheim added.

It wasn't relief so much as incredulity. 'Well, of course, I'm disappointed about the other scripts –' he began.

'They were crap.'

'– but I'm thrilled you like the, erm, Millhouse script.' He managed to grab the name as it flashed to the back of his memory. His team were looking stunned, which didn't help. 'Actually, it's a movie I've been developing on my own. I just threw it into the pot at the last minute,' he elaborated.

'And a good thing you did or your ass would've been out that door.'

'What's its name again?' A bemused looking Dylan Tizer asked.

'*Untitled*. Stupid title, Carmichael.'

'It's just a working title,' Mitch assured him. He heaved a huge inward sigh of relief. His job was safe. He might yet get through this meeting. But how long could he survive? He wondered. And that was only one of several questions rampaging through his mind, none of which he had any of the answers to.

CHAPTER SIX

Milly could picture Jonson sprawled in his lounge, with the phone clamped to his ear. She could hear him flicking through the mail. A book-club offer, a new wonder credit card, the gas bill and a Reader's Digest superdraw probably.

'Nothing, really. Yesterday we had a rock band called Venom check in.'

'Venom? Never heard of 'em. Mind you . . .' He yawned long and loud.

'You sound knackered,' she said.

'I am. Jet-lagged. Been to New York, remember.'

'You should try to stay up today.'

'No way. As soon as this phone's down, I'm pushing out some Zs.'

'What about tonight, then?' she asked. 'I thought you could come to mine. I'll get George and David round for a takeaway. Say eight o'clock.'

'Great. Night-night, Milly.'

'You'll be sorry.'

A night in with his mates wasn't something Jonson was looking forward to. He was exhausted, he hadn't read her script and, worse still, he couldn't even find it. The last time he'd definitely seen it had been on the outbound flight. He'd spoken with the airline, but they hadn't found it. She could print off another, of course, but that wasn't the issue. Not reading it was bad, but losing it was unforgivable. Perhaps his only saving grace was that the whole trip had been a disaster. He was in the shit, and there was no getting away from it.

It was fortunate for Mitch that Willenheim didn't like meetings to drag on, but before the big man left the boardroom he asked about the ownership of the Millhouse script.

'Absolutely, sir. Four-year option on it,' Mitch said. He had now well and truly taken the plunge. He was treading water with no shallow end and no way of getting out. How long could he last? Long enough, he hoped, to complete his *Mission Impossible*. He couldn't take much confidence from the confused faces of the people in the room. He could see that Dylan Tizer, head of Legal, was still trying hard to recall a four-year option contract on a movie he'd never heard of.

As soon as Willenheim had left Mitch muttered an excuse and fled to avoid the volley of enquiries levelled at him as if he were a lawyer leaving a courtroom. He wasn't being rude. He wanted answers as much as they did, but in his case his career depended on them. He shut his office door behind him and breathed out slowly. Had he just been presented with a huge problem or a huge opportunity? He didn't know, but he was aware of how lucky he'd been. His six scripts had been metaphorically torn up, like spent lottery tickets, and by rights he should have been fired, but God had taken pity on him and plonked an angel called Juliet Millhouse in his lap. Her script had jammed the guillotine.

But who the hell was Juliet Millhouse? How had Willenheim got hold of her script? Did I give it to him? Have I ever seen one called *Untitled*? Not that it mattered. It could have fallen out of the sky for all he cared.

His office door burst open and his urgent team marched in, led by Scott, and gathered around him. They looked like a clutch of newly hatched chicks with their beaks agape, waiting for something that their mother was about to regurgitate.

'I thought that went well,' Mitch said blandly.

'Not, perhaps, what we'd expected, though,' Scott said.

'Maybe. Disappointing about the other scripts. We've got a lot of writers and producers to let down this morning. Josie, would you line up my calls with their agents this morning?' Mitch asked.

'Sure.'

'Okay. So we can reconvene later?'

If he thought they were just going to leave right then he was plain naive. Now they looked bitterly disappointed, as if the mother bird had been away gorging herself on fresh salmon and had returned to the nest and done nothing more than burped.

'Mitch.' Claudia folded her arms aggressively – he knew what was coming. 'Who is Juliet Millhouse?'

'Yeah, Mitch, what the hell's going on?'

'I can't believe you haven't mentioned her before now.'

Mitch thought frantically. 'Look, Juliet is a young

writer out of New York whom I met at a writing course I took in New York State. It was way before most of you joined me here. Anyway, she wrote this script and sent it in and I helped her with its development. On a teaching basis more than a professional one. I only included it in Willenheim's pile because he wanted warm stories. It wasn't ready, but I figured we had nothing to lose. Believe me, at the meeting I was as surprised as you were. I got lucky. But thank God I did, huh?'

His team digested the story.

'Who's her agent?' Claudia asked, clearly unconvinced by his explanation.

'Is that relevant right now?'

Answering a question with a question. A sure sign of guilt!

'I think so.'

He knew that he couldn't cope with an interrogation, so he changed tack. 'It sounds, Claudia, as if you don't believe me. And I do not appreciate having my word called into question. Would you like me to get her on the phone so you can speak with her?'

'No,' she said – to his relief.

'Now does anyone else have any other doubts?' They shook their heads. 'Good. So, I have some calls to make . . .' Dismissed, his team began to file out of his office. 'Scott, could I have a word, please?'

Scott shut the door with a wry smile. 'You don't know who she is, do you?'

'Not a fucking clue.'

Both men laughed.

'Was it that obvious?'

'Not until the angry speech. Classic guilt reaction, man. How's all this happened?'

'I've no idea.'

'Wow,' Scott said. 'So, we have to find the lady.'

'You bet your ass we do. First we'll check with Records about scripts received. Do any come in that I don't see?'

'Certainly not the ones that get as far as Willenheim. The only ones we don't see are unsolicited and they're sent back unread.'

'But they still get recorded, right?'

'Sure.'

'So check those too – and all the in-house and freelance readers. Do it quietly, though – no one must know we're searching for her. The fewer people who know about this, the more chance we've got of getting away with it.'

'What about Claudia?'

'I'll deal with her.'

'Good of you to get this,' Georgina said, taking some plates out of Milly's oven as Milly carefully arranged the aluminium containers on a tray. 'Sorry again for the other night.'

'He sent flowers, you know.'

'Oh dear.'

Milly and Georgina had met at Leeds University and had been inseparable ever since. They'd shared a flat together for six years, and only their respective weddings could have split them up, until Milly's collapsed. Georgina moved into her flat for almost two months and practically nursed her back to health, but it was David who became the real hero of the hour. He and Elliot were really only ever friends by association and hadn't seen each other since, which was understandable given what had happened. One night, Elliot pitched up at the flat unannounced to retrieve the remainder of his belongings. He had enough good sense to leave his current girlfriend in the car, but not enough not to boast to David about what was waiting for him downstairs. Every man has his limits and David had just discovered his – he promptly broke Elliot's jaw.

'Shit,' Milly huffed, 'they haven't put coconut rice in. They always forget one thing. What was it last time?' She thought. 'No ribs.'

'It's probably not their fault. David may not have ordered it. He's mad at the moment.'

'Oh.'

'Whatever you do, don't mention that bloody football match.'

'Why? Did they lose?'

'No, worse than that, he got substituted. Never seen him so pissed off as when he got in. And then he had to perform for me, poor thing. It was my fourteen-day window.'

'Well, that must have cheered him up, then.'

'You're joking. We'd already done it in the morning and the night before.'

Milly chuckled. 'Poor old David. Did he manage?'

'Put it this way, it was a good job he was taken off.'

Giggling, Milly carried the food through to her sitting room, where David was organising their drinks and Jonson was sprawled on her sofa.

'You all right there, Jonson?' David asked sarcastically.

'Aiee. Horrendously jet-lagged person lying here.'

'Well then, you shouldn't have slept all day, should you,' Milly chipped in. He hadn't mentioned her film script yet and she was worried that he hadn't liked it.

Jonson joined them at the table. 'So come on, then. How was your trip? What happened to you?' David asked.

'Hang on. I've got something to tell Milly and I need to say it now.'

'Oh! Blimey. You're not going to propose, are you?'

'Shut up, will ya? I've got bad news. Well . . . it's more unfortunate, really, but you'll probably think it's bad.'

'Right, well come on then. Let's have it.'

'Before I tell you, you should know that I also have some really good news.'

'Just get on with it.'

'I haven't read your script.'

'Is that it?'

'Yeah.'

'I can't believe you. Two seven-hour flights and you still didn't have time.'

'No. One flight.'

'Oh, right. You swam back. Well, fair enough.'

'Milly. I lost it.'

'But you're a personal courier! I take it you didn't lose your package as well.'

'No. 'Course not.'

'Oh, thanks a *lot*.'

Milly wasn't really that disappointed but pretended to be anyway.

'I don't see how I can get fed up with my agent if my mates can't even read it.'

'Has he not read it yet?' Georgina asked.

Milly just looked at her.

'Have you spoken to him about it?'

'Oh, yeah, we speak every day. I can't get him off the phone. No, of course I haven't spoken to him.'

'Bloke's an arsehole,' David chipped in. 'I read it last night. Absolutely loved it.'

'I didn't know you'd read it.' Milly beamed.

Jonson moaned. 'Nice one, Dave. Thanks a lot. I feel even worse now.'

'So you should,' Georgina said.

'I'm sorry, Milly. Are you upset?'

'Depends on what your good news is.'

Jonson's face instantly became animated. 'You ain't going to believe what happened to me in New York.'

'This needs to be good.'

'Immigration had a problem with my passport photo.'

''Cos of the bandaged head?'

'Yeah. So I explain what happened to my head and they let me through. But then this Customs geezer's giving me the once-over. Asks me where I'm from, where I'm going, you know, that kind of stuff. He's really polite, but it's obvious he's got me down as dodgy and he asks me if I'd mind being searched. I'm, like, no problem, 'cos I know I ain't got anything to hide, right? So he leads me into this room.'

'Not strip-searched?' Milly said, hands over her face.

'Hang on. So I go into this room and there's two blokes waiting for me and the biggest fucking dog you've ever seen in your life. At first, I thought it was a horse . . .'

Jonson hated dogs. His mum had once had a terrier from the RSPCA and Jonson could well understand why it needed rescuing from its previous owner.

'. . . and it's having a good mooch round but I don't care because I've got nothing to hide, right? And the bastard dog only goes and freaks out, doesn't it?'

'Why?'

'Dunno. But it's barking the place down, like it's found a smoking crack bomb sticking out of my arse.'

David sniggered at the imagery. 'Is there any coconut rice?'

'So I strip down to my boxers, and they're poring over my clothes and the dog's still freaking out. Any minute I'm expecting the you-know-what.'

'The gloves.'

'Exactly. But somehow I'm spared all that. They put it down to residues, so they have to let me go.'

'Poor you.'

'But that's not all,' Jonson said. 'So, anyway, I run to the arrivals lounge and there's my driver waiting for me looking well pissed off. I mean, it's like an hour since we landed and everyone else on my flight had been through.'

'What did you tell him?'

'That I'd fainted. It would have looked well iffy to say I'd been searched for drugs.'

Jonson had not known how seriously Americans took their healthcare, or how litigious they were when it came to professional injuries. His driver had radioed ahead to inform the company that their courier had collapsed and they had insisted he was thoroughly examined by their own physician. 'So there I am, right. I haven't been off the plane more than two hours, and I'm next to naked again in another little room with another total stranger. They wouldn't let me fly for twenty-four hours. That's why I'm late getting back.'

This could only happen to Jonson, Milly thought, and giggled.

'So am I forgiven or what?'

'Once you've read it. I'll run you off another copy.'

'Hey, no problem. Bring it on.'

For the second morning running, Mitch didn't need his alarm. By the time it sounded, he was wrapped in his dressing gown, having just been thrashed around violently in his new eight-head power shower. Scott was still asleep on the sofa: he had stayed the night after a futile search for their mystery writer. Records had nothing on the name or the title, and their speculative calls to the major literary agencies also drew a blank. Scott had crashed out around one, leaving Mitch to continue on the Internet. Now Mitch made some coffee and put a cup beside him, which roused him.

'What time is it?' he mumbled.

'Just after eight,' Mitch lied.

'Did you find anything on the Net?'

'No.' Another shaft of panic shot through Mitch. This screenplay was hot property, not just because a studio head had loved it but because it was still available, unsigned. That made it incredibly hot. A race was on for this woman's signature and soon no one would be able to see for waving cheque books, all desperate for her greedy scrawl on their dotted line. How quickly the rumour spread was down to how they conducted their search, but time wasn't on their side. They had to proceed cautiously, and it wasn't just a matter of calling up the likes of the William Morris Agency and asking the receptionist whether any of their agents represented a Juliet Millhouse. Agents were dangerous: they had a highly developed sense of smell for opportunities and rats.

When Mitch and Scott reached the office it was still early and Dolores' office was locked.

'Still, it was worth a try,' Mitch said. It had been over-optimistic to think it might be open with the script lying on the desk. Mitch had been wondering all night how he could ask Dolores for a copy of a script that had supposedly emerged from his office in the first place, and had come up with nothing she wouldn't see through immediately.

'*Dolores, hi. Could I have a copy of that Millhouse script?*'

'*Why? Don't you have your own?*'

'*Er, yeah. Yeah, of course I do, but mine's at home.*'

'*You only have one copy! Your associates haven't got copies. You haven't registered it with Records. The legal department, who drew up the contract, they haven't got a copy. You don't have a development computer file copy. You . . .*'

'*Yes, yes, all right, you fucking witch. Forget I ever mentioned it.*'

'So what now?' Scott asked.

'We try the East Coast agents this morning and the

smaller ones on the West Coast. We check with television credits on sit-coms, gag writers, comedy-writing workshops. Her name has to show up somewhere.'

'And if it doesn't?'

'Shit, Scott, could you sound any more defeatist?'

'Sorry.'

'If we get nothing out of all this, we'll get the team in and brainstorm some ideas.'

'Sure. We'll find her.'

'And she's bound to have an agent.'

'Well, yeah. You'd think so.'

'So they'll find us. They must have a record of which studio they sent it to. If this script's so fucking good, the agent should be bashing our doors down. Right.'

Lyal was having a great Wednesday afternoon. Dylan Walsh, one of his 'always gets through' clients, had opened a new play in the West End to rave reviews. Ben Harper, a young actors' agent, had stopped by to congratulate Lyal on his success, but it wasn't the play that Lyal wanted to talk about. At the opening night, he'd flirted terribly with the theatre's press officer and he was altogether smitten.

'I'm telling you, Ben. She was totally gorgeous,' Lyal boasted as casually as he could. Every Monday morning he had to endure Ben's tales of his weekend debauchery, leaving him to bitterly reflect on his Sunday, typically spent at an Adventure Barn with his kids, and later that evening having a wank in the bath while his wife ordered the weekly shop over the Internet.

'Hello, Juliet. How are you?' said Muriel.

'Fine. You?'

'Oh, much the same. Are you wanting Lyal? Hang on, I'll just see if he's free.' She clicked off and eased Milly into the pause zone with 'Greensleeves' for company.

It had been a week since Milly had last phoned, so she felt well within her rights to be calling him again. Muriel craned her neck to see if she could catch Lyal's eye; he was now replicating a woman's figure with his hands.

Lyal was aware that his assistant was flagging him but she wasn't using the code to indicate that it was a Premier League client with a call he wanted to take, so he dismissed her with a minimal gesture.

'I'm sorry, Juliet. He's tied up at the moment.' Muriel was back on the line. 'Can I give him a message for you?'

'Not really,' Milly said. 'It's just that I wondered whether he'd had a chance to take a look at my screenplay yet. And, if so, whether I could come in to discuss it.' Exactly the same message as I left last week, Milly raged, and hit the red button on her mobile. 'Give him the same message pad, why don't you? Just change the date!' she told the phone.

Georgina pushed Milly's latte towards her. They were in one of the few independent cafés left in Mayfair. Milly had just read the environmentalists' bible, *No Logo*, by Naomi Klein, and had decided to boycott the famous coffee chains as a result. Georgina hadn't read it, and neither did she intend to if it meant she couldn't enjoy a milky coffee in a crushed velvet lounger at Starbucks.

'Still hasn't read it,' she said.

'Muriel didn't know. Which means he hasn't.'

'Did you speak to him?'

'No. Of course I didn't. Don't keep asking that. I don't get to speak to him.' She said it as if he were the Wizard of Oz.

'How long has it been now?'

'Five months,' Georgina tutted. 'Bloke is a total arse-hole.'

'Is he?'

'Yes. That screenplay of yours is fabulous and has every right to be considered and if he won't read it, then that's what he is.'

Milly was staring glumly at the little brown lumps of melted sugar in the bowl. Georgina reached over and touched her hand. 'What's up, Milly?' she asked gently.

'Oh, I dunno. I'm not sure I've got the energy for this any more. I certainly can't go through all that stuff I went through with *Artistic Licence* again.'

'Is it just Lyal?'

'It's everything, really. My job sucks and I've never got any money, and before you say it, this isn't because I need a shag, okay?'

Georgina held up her hands. 'Would I say that?' she joked.

'You see, most people change jobs, take up a sport or, yes, meet another man, but it's always something realistic. Me, I've chosen the road marked "Hollywood". Ridiculous!'

'There's nothing wrong in having a dream.'

'So long as that's not all you've got. Little girls want to marry princes, but they grow out of it. I'm thirty-two and relying on a fairytale to provide me with my happy ending.'

Georgina was silent for a moment.

'Come on, Milly,' she said eventually. 'This isn't like you. It is tough I know. But I also know that you get back from life what you put into it. You know, reap what you sow and all that. And I don't know why, but I've got a gut feeling about this.'

'It's probably just your diet,' Milly joked, forcing herself to smile.

'No I have, seriously. You can't give up now. You've worked too hard and besides, none of us will let you anyway.'

She appreciated her friend's kind words and desperately wanted to believe them and they did make her feel a little better. The iceberg of frustration receded a little until it was submerged at least.

CHAPTER SEVEN

After another fruitless day spent searching through his haystack for the elusive needle, Mitch explained his predicament to his team – except Claudia – although he referred to it as their opportunity. It was disappointing for them that the script had gone from an exciting sure thing to a doubtful long-shot, but they were all keen to help him.

This morning Mitch drove through the studio gates just as he heard the first chords of his favourite record on the radio. Typical. In a twenty-minute journey he'd suffered irrelevant traffic reports, inane banter and even an Osmonds track – not one decent tune until now. He hoped this wasn't an omen for the rest of the day.

He slammed his car door and locked it. There was no need to pull up the hood: any car thieves who got into the compound would be shot and it never rained in LA.

'Hey, Mitch.'

It was a voice he thought he recognised and he spun round. It was Ron Green, a very senior vice-president of something or other. Mitch had hardly ever spoken to him.

'Great work on that script, Mitch. Whatever it is, it must be hot.'

Thanks a lot, pal. Don't happen to know who the author is, do you? 'Thanks a lot,' he said. What else *could* he say?

'I haven't seen Albert so excited since *Rain Man*. Way to go, Mitch.'

'Thanks, Ron.'

This was the only advantage he could find in his predicament: he was the star of the studio, the man of the moment, the Boy Wonder, the suit with the killer scripts. It was exactly what he'd worked so hard for so long to achieve. Only he couldn't enjoy it. He felt like an Olympic gold medallist parading around the track draped in his national flag only to spot a party of men in white coats holding a piss-pot and remembering that his urine was loaded with cheetah hormones.

'Morning, Mitch. How are you?' asked a seductive-looking receptionist who had never spoken to him before. 'Is there anything I can do for you today?' Her eyelids were batting at him like shutters in a storm while her collagen-enhanced lips pouted seductively. Everyone wanted a slice of him now, Mitch reflected. Ordinarily, as a single man, he would have been salivating, but his brain was incommunicado with his groin. His mind was on only one woman and he couldn't care less what she looked like, as long as her name was Juliet Millhouse.

He made his way quickly through the building, eager to avoid any of Willenheim's immediate staff, or even the man himself. When he reached his office, he was both suspicious and relieved to note Claudia's absence, and convened an impromptu meeting with his team.

Scott closed Mitch's office door and went to sit down beside Josie and Karl.

'Thanks, Scott. Day three. Before we get into it, does

anyone have any news?' A stupid question – if they had, he'd have heard it by now. 'Okay, let's recap. Records have nothing, ditto the freelance readers. As far as we can tell, she doesn't have an agent, and there's no Juliet Millhouse out there in TV land.'

Mitch rubbed his eyes. 'Shit. Who writes a script and sends it in with no contact details?' he asked no one in particular.

'Maybe she doesn't want it to get made,' Josie offered tentatively.

'What?'

'I don't know. I just thought maybe she's not interested in Hollywood.'

'So why send it in?'

'To make a point?' Josie suggested.

Mitch thought about this for a moment. 'Nah, that's bullshit.'

'But Josie might be right,' Scott said. 'What if she's one of these hippie chicks, a Seattle tree-hugger type who doesn't agree with "Hollywood man"?'

'So what do you all suggest? That we run a check on all eco-warriors? Most of them haven't got social-security numbers and live in tunnels under roads. They'll be *so* easy to find.'

The three looked suitably chastised.

'We have to work on the theory that she can be found – or I might as well go now and show my bare ass to Willenheim so he can kick it down Hollywood Boulevard. She might be a hippie chick – that's fine. She's almost certainly weird, but that's fine too. As far as we can tell, she's never been produced, right?'

Everyone nodded in general agreement.

'So then she'll be as desperate as we are, right?'

Suddenly the door burst open and in stomped a furious-looking Claudia. 'I wasn't aware there was a meeting this morning, Mitch,' she snapped.

'More of a get-together, really. You haven't missed much.'

'When are we going to get a copy of this script? I can't wait to read it.'

'All in good time.'

'Is there any reason for the hold-up? So many people keep asking for it.'

'Just finalising a few details. That's all.'

Mitch felt he still had the upper hand, but he didn't like the smirk that had appeared on her perfect little face. When he finally got his hands on a copy of the script, he was going to shove it up her ass. That was a motivating vision.

'I've just been talking about the script with Dolores . . .' Claudia's smirk widened and Mitch tensed.

'Oh?' he said.

'Yeah. We had a good old chat. Actually, she's a little pissed.'

'Oh dear.' Mitch's eyelid twitched and he sensed that his composure was about to desert him.

'Yeah. She can't get hold of you so she asked me to pass on a message.' She left a tantalising pause. 'Mr Willenheim would like to see you.'

Mr Mahmood added the photo of Venom grouped around himself to his office wall of fame. It was in pride of place above his desk, sandwiched between Frank Sinatra and Liza Minnelli and just below the Queen. *We have five stars outside the hotel and as many stars as possible inside.*

A celebrity in residence at the hotel was simply the best advertisement it could muster – if it's good enough for Clint Eastwood, it's good enough for me – but it was always difficult to strike the right balance between trying to exploit their presence and not pissing them off. Before a star's arrival, a member of their entourage would usually call to check details, and to emphasise their employer's need for privacy. No one must know that the star was in residence.

Of course, this was ludicrous. No one must know – apart from the twenty or so media teams lined up for interviews by the record company, or whoever was paying. Michael Jackson's visit to London in 1987 was a good example and, for Mr Mahmood, a particularly painful memory.

The superstar had been booked into the Shelton Tower but it turned out to be a decoy booking to create an even greater media frenzy. While the king of pop relaxed at the Dorchester, Mr Mahmood, incandescent with rage, looked like an extra from his *Thriller* video. For a whole ten days, every television bulletin and newspaper reminded him of his personal humiliation. And to compound his misery, the vacant suite was filled by the New Kids on the Block, kicking off their ill-fated come-back. By this time, however, they were NKOTB and no one CGAS – could give a shit.

Today Milly and the rest of the staff were gathered in Mr Mahmood's office for his daily pep talk.

'So . . . pliss you mustt all remember what a fine hotele this is. It is the finest hotele in Londonne and you should be proud of itt and of yourselves. Yess.'

General nodding and yawn-suppressing.

'Rememberr, the finest hotele in Londonne. So, one of the finest hoteles in the worlde. No?'

Milly would have loved to have argued both of those points with him. Finest hotel in London? No. One of the finest hotels in the world? Certainly not. The most committed hotel manager in the world? Absolutely. No doubt about that whatsoever.

'Any questions?' Mr Mahmood asked. There never were, and his troops were sent out into the field to honour and serve.

It was a wet Wednesday morning, and Samson was busy making hay. It was generally accepted that Samson would never retire. He would most likely croak on the job carrying some Louis Vuitton luggage into the lobby, and earning surely his greatest tip ever.

Milly arrived back at her desk ready to face the onslaught. 'Any shafts of business enlightenment that might help me through the day?' Lucas asked. He hadn't been at the meeting.

'Be proud of your hotel and of yourself.'

'Oh, right,' he said, in an attempt at irony. Then he noticed a man approaching the reception desk. You'll have to deal with this bloke. I checked him in, and he's a pain in the arse.'

'I vant to change rooms,' the man snapped. He didn't look as if he could be humoured. He had yellowing grey hair, and a heavily lined face with broken veins. Milly didn't know his name.

'My room iz not acceptable,' he went on.

'I'm sorry to hear that, sir. Which room is it?'

'Zree eight zree.'

Milly hastily consulted her screen. 'Let's see . . . Mr Voller. What is the problem with it?'

'It is too noisy and it stinks.'

Noise was a common problem for hotels near Hyde Park Corner, but not one the staff could do much about – you want to stay on Park Lane overlooking the park, that means you'll have to put up with the noise from cars delivering other fat wallets such as yourself. *Hello, Scotland Yard? Mr Voller has decided to take an afternoon nap. Would you mind awfully shutting down Park Lane? I'm sure Londoners will understand. It won't be the first time a German has brought our great capital to a standstill.*

'I'm sorry about that, sir.' Milly gave him her best smile. The noise problem could only be solved by allocating a room at the back of the hotel. This completely cut out the noise, but unfortunately the view as well. You want views, you have noise. You don't want noise, you can't have views. It was a simple choice.

'You said your room smells, sir.'

'No. I zaid it stinks.'

Mr Mahmood would have been proud of the way Milly absorbed the insult as if it hadn't been uttered.

'What does it smell of, Mr Voller?'

'Tobacco.' At that moment he blew out a plume of cigar smoke. She wanted to laugh. Well fancy that. She'd had this complaint many times, although never from someone while they were actually smoking, but the irony seemed lost on Mr Voller. That he smoked was irrelevant because it wasn't the smell of his tobacco that was annoying him: it was the smoke from the room's previous occupant to which he was referring.

'I'm so sorry to hear that, Mr Voller. I'll just see which other rooms might be more suitable for you.' The words almost stuck in her throat. Fancy the room smelling of smoke when people like you suck off the only lucrative part of Cuba each waking hour.

'Here we are, sir. I have a room on the east side of the hotel, which is very quiet. It is a smoking room, but I'm sure it won't smell like the other one. I'll give you a key-card now and I can arrange for your belongings to be transferred.'

'I will still see the park, no?'

Milly smiled and didn't reply. After all, he'd answered his own question.

'The customer is always right' is the mantra of business throughout the world, and one with which Milly was becoming increasingly bored.

A resolute but inwardly quaking Mitch made his way to Willenheim's office suite. He carried with him the tacit support of his team, whose fervour for the task in hand had doubled with Claudia's announcement. Ordinarily he would have asked her what Willenheim wanted, but in this instance it was obvious. He would also have liked to have asked what Claudia had been doing with Dolores in the first place, but he knew the answer to that too: applying for his job.

It seemed everyone was still keen to be associated with Mitch Carmichael.

'Hey, Mitch, how ya doing? Sean Clayton. Accounts.'

Sean had never felt the need to introduce himself before now. Mitch was still the studio's hero. He felt like a restaurant special, a dish that everyone wants today but which tomorrow will be gone. History! Just chalk dust at the bottom of a board, replaced by something even more special, Chicken Claudia perhaps.

He entered Willenheim's palatial quarters. Dolores sat behind a granite desk at the end of the reception area. She didn't just organise the man, she guarded him.

'Hello, Dolores,' he sang, to demonstrate how confident and happy he was feeling today. But Dolores could smell an injured animal and wasn't fooled. Without looking up from her desk, she pointed silently to a chair with her chubby index finger.

Dolores was the best PA in the business. She had to be, because no one quite as unsightly as her could have got on in Hollywood without being brilliant at something. She had no neck, so her blotchy face appeared to emerge straight from her vast, square torso. And what a face it was: her eyes were sunk into her head like pebbles in concrete, her nose was short and bulbous, emerging from her hairy cheeks. It was a face that could frighten anyone, especially embattled and beleaguered development executives.

Mitch sat down, determined to engage her in conversation. She didn't look as if she was in a particularly good mood – but how could he know that? He wasn't sure that her facial muscles could configure 'happy'. It wasn't a comforting thought, but he was desperate and Dolores was the only person who could save him. She had access to the script.

He took a deep breath. He needed his charm now as he never had before. It had served him so well in his heyday, but he hadn't faced such insurmountable odds as these.

'Are you busy, Dolores?' Could he have asked a more boring question? It was hardly the opening salvo he'd been looking for. Dolores obviously agreed: she didn't bother to reply.

He tried again. 'Have you read the script, Dolores?'

Much better. She actually looked at him.

'We get a lot of scripts through here.'

'Yeah. Of course. I meant the Millhouse script. Have you read it?'

'Yeah. Have you?'

Her question hit him like a medicine ball.

'Me?' Mitch gulped.

'Do you see anyone else in the room? Yeah. You.'

'Of *course*. I developed it.'

'Oh, really?' She suddenly seemed keen for their conversation to continue.

Shit. If only I'd kept my trap shut.

'Mitch, is that you out there?' Willenheim bellowed from his room.

Mitch had never been happier to hear his boss's voice, and he jumped to attention. The big man appeared at his door smiling, ready to welcome in his Sir Lancelot. They shook hands and Mitch was dragged from the reception frying pan into the office fire.

One thing was certain: he hadn't been summoned to be shot, and that was a relief.

'So, how's it all going? I haven't heard from you about the script. That's good news, right?'

'Absolutely.'

'Great!' Willenheim said triumphantly. 'I've got a good feeling about this movie.'

'So do I, sir.'

'Where are we with it?'

Mitch steadied himself. Improvising and lying with his boss wasn't his idea of fun. 'I think the script could do with one more pass.'

'Really? Why? I think it's great as it is. Don't tinker for the sake of it. I know what you guys are like. You wanna claim it as your own work. Take my advice, this script is ready.'

'Yes, sir.'

'Let's get a director on board and shoot the fucking thing.'

'Absolutely.' Mitch nearly passed out.

'Hollywood takes too long – it takes too long to make *pictures*! Hell, we've got the script so let's go ahead and make it. I'm green-lighting this all the way.'

This was the speech that Mitch had dreamed of Willenheim making but not under these circumstances. Now it was a nightmare. He'd never seen Willenheim like this before. He was acting like a grandpa about to take his grandchild fishing. This script had changed the man entirely. He seemed so excited and full of life, but this wasn't good news: it was frightening.

'I keep thinking of that irritating guy on the plane laughing so hard. It reminded me what our business is all about. I watch a movie and I don't laugh any more. I just think about what box office it could do. Sitting next to that asshole on the plane reminded me what it is that I do. Hell, I entertain the world. This script is going to make one hell of a movie. People will love it. Great characters and a great fucking story. That's what people want, right?'

'Yes, sir. Totally.'

'I mean, I don't laugh at movies any more. But, hell, I laughed at this script!'

'You did?'

'Hell, yeah. Right from the beginning when his head goes up. And it made me feel so good at the end I nearly goddamn cried.'

Mitch had a good idea that it would be making him cry soon also, but for different reasons. He was racking his brain for the right question to ask. Something to unlock some information – anything that might help him. 'Well, I'm glad you feel that way, sir,' he muttered weakly.

'Call me Albert.'

Mitch nearly fell off his chair. At this rate, they'd be in Willenheim's hot tub together this evening having a beer.

'Well, Albert, it's great to know you're so behind me on this.'

'Hey, let me tell ya, I'm right up your ass on it. What's the writer like?'

'Albert' was full of surprises today. Usually studio

chiefs couldn't have been less interested in writers.

'Oh, she's real smart.'

'Attractive?'

'Er. Kind of. Not my type but, yeah, I guess. Hey, who cares, huh?'

'I'd like to meet her.' Willenheim was smiling from ear to ear. 'Set up a meeting with Dolores, why don't you?'

This was a joke. First he loves the movie, then he announces it's changed his life and now he wants to meet the writer. Studio heads never meet writers. The only writers Willenheim ever meets are waiting on him in restaurants. 'You'd like to *meet* her?'

'Sure. Why not?'

Mitch mustered just enough emotional energy from some reserve batteries he had lying in a drawer somewhere to contort his face into a smile of agreement.

'By the way, I'm having lunch with Ang Lee today, I might get him to take a look.'

Hey, why not? I like pressure. I can take more. Just keep piling it on. Tell you what. Let's play a game: see how much pressure Mitch can take before he shoots himself.

'Set it up with Dolores.'

'Oh, right. Yeah.'

Willenheim was out of his chair and on his way over to shake Mitch's hand. The meeting was over and he'd survived. But it felt like a stay of execution.

CHAPTER EIGHT

Although the hotel was busy, Milly's afternoon had dragged. From the look of Samson's sodden shoulders it was still raining, and a metaphorical cloud had settled right over her head. She didn't suffer from depression, just the occasional dark mood, which rarely lasted more than a day, but those days were bad, with no limits to the depths of despair she might plumb.

Mr Voller had sparked off her gloom but he hadn't caused it. That honour was Lyal's. In spite of Lucas's best efforts, the mood showed no signs of lifting. It was like a train waiting for its guard. She was fed up with being ignored by Lyal and her patience was all but exhausted. On her way to work this morning, as the doors of the Piccadilly line train finally snapped shut, like a clasp on an overfilled sports bag, she'd promised herself she wouldn't call. But then Mr Voller happened, the inner anger welled, and before she knew it she was back in the pause zone.

'He's just taken another call, Juliet. Is there any message?' Muriel asked. At least, Milly assumed she was speaking, but it might have been a recorded message. *Yes. Could you tell him I think he's a useless little worm?* 'No, Muriel. Just tell him I rang, would you?'

'Yes, of course, dear.'

*   *   *

An excited Jonson ran up the marble steps of the Shelton Tower, Park Lane, at precisely the right moment. He timed his entrances to avoid Samson and the other doormen. No way was he tipping a man for holding open a door. He saw Milly straight away, directing a man towards the lifts. Even when she spotted Jonson she didn't smile.

This was a challenge, which he immediately accepted. 'Good afternoon, madam,' he said. 'My name is Jonson Clarke. I used to be your good friend and I could always make you smile . . .'

'Hi, Jonson. Hang on.' She had a word with Lucas, then slipped out from behind the desk and walked towards the Park Bar, beckoning to Jonson to join her.

A new barman called Halim was serving, fresh from Mr Mahmood's crash course in servility. 'Good afternoon, Miss Milly. What can I get you?'

She had abandoned her efforts to get him to drop the miss.

'We'll just have a beer, please, and a mineral water.'

'Still or sparkling?'

'Still is fine. Thank you, Halim.'

'I will bring them over for you, Miss Milly.'

She flopped into the sofa in a corner of the room. It was where she always sat with either Jonson or Georgina and it was her one act of defiance to Mr Mahmood. Staff were not allowed to entertain their friends or family in the hotel during working hours, but as hers were practically all the available hours in her life it was a rule she ignored and, remarkably, Mr Mahmood seemed happy to waive it for her.

'You look happy, Jonson. You had good news or something?'

'Kind of.'

'Lucky you. Wish I had.'

You didn't need to be one of her three closest friends to understand the mood she was in but Jonson prided himself on being the best person to sort her out.

'I see you've got the bandages off.'

'Yeah, 'bout time.'

'Will it grow back?'

'They don't think so.'

'You could always go for the comb-over.' She laughed.

It was a breakthrough in shifting her mood, but Jonson was now thoroughly fed up with hair jokes, and this one fell as flat as the water she'd ordered.

'Sorry, Jonson.'

'I didn't come here to talk about my head.'

'So, what's the good news, then?'

'Haven't you got anything to ask me?'

Milly thought for a moment. She didn't think she had. 'What?'

Halim came over and placed their drinks on the table. 'Thank you, Halim. Come on, Jonson, spit it out.'

He was disappointed in her. 'What I thought of your film, of course!'

She smiled – not a huge smile but it was progress. He was trying to make up for his New York fiasco. She looked at him fondly. He was like an excited teenager about to tell a policeman what he had seen. 'Okay, then. What did you think?'

'I loved it. I didn't think I was so funny.'

'Well, you are, and thank God for it.'

'Seriously, Milly, it's fucking brilliant.'

'Thanks,' was all she said.

'Don't thank me. Thank you. You're going to make me a star. I was laughing out loud at things that actually happened to *me*. Will I get a credit?'

But he couldn't raise another smile – or even a response at all. If anything, his eulogising about the script only made Milly feel worse. Everyone who'd read it so far had loved it, but the one person who she really needed to read it wasn't so inclined.

'Shit, Milly, if I'd known my opinion meant this much to you, I wouldn't have bothered.'

'Don't say that. It means everything to me. Shit, without you that screenplay wouldn't exist.'

'So what's up, then?'

'It's just . . . oh, I don't know. Nothing.'

'He hasn't read it, has he?'

She looked at him dolefully.

'He hasn't read it yet!' Jonson echoed in disgust which was a bit rich coming from him.

'No.'

'Well, he's an arsehole, then! A total fucking chump.'

'That's what Georgina said.'

'And she's right – although it pains me to say so. So what are you going to do?'

'About what?'

'About the arsehole.'

'There's not a lot I can do. I can't *make* him read it.'

'Well, it's his loss.'

Milly laughed. How many times had she imagined that

her script turned out to be Lyal's loss?

'Yeah. And you're better off without him.' Jonson was warming to his theme.

'You figure?'

'Absolutely. Have you called him?'

What a stupid question! It was on a par with 'Have you plugged it in?'

'Well then, you should sack him.'

Milly laughed again. 'If only.'

'Ring 'im and tell 'im that if he doesn't read it by the end of the week, you'll take it elsewhere.'

She shook her head.

'Why not? You keep going on and on about how crap he is.'

'It's not as simple as that.'

'Yeah, it is – all right, listen. I know nothing about the film world, yeah, but this isn't about the film world, this is about life. And you're too nice.'

'*What?*'

'Yeah. That's it. You're too nice.'

'What's that got to do with anything?'

'The way you treat people! You want people to like you.'

'So?' she said, sounding defensive. 'There's nothing wrong with wanting to be liked.'

'No, of course not, but that's why this twat treats you like shit. Because he can. 'Cos he knows you're going to put up with it. It's what he gets off on.'

Milly was vanquished, because Jonson was one hundred per cent accurate, as he well knew.

'Do you think he treats all his clients like you?' he asked warmly.

Milly shook her head.

'Fucking right he doesn't. The big ones, his earners, they probably treat him like shit. They give him earache, which he has to wear. He won't like it, but he can't do anything about it 'cos he needs 'em, see?'

'Yeah, I can see *that*. And he doesn't need me.'

'Yes, he does. He just doesn't realise it yet 'cos he ain't read it. He does fucking need you. He just doesn't rate you and he doesn't respect you. But you have to earn that from him.'

'How?'

'By taking him on. Shit, you've done the hard bit – that was writing a bloody great film script. There must be loads of crap scripts out there – there *must* be, 'cos look at all the crap films they make!'

Milly laughed unwillingly.

'You keep going on and on about this *game* you're playing with him, so you have to start playing rough. Unless you stand up to this bloke, he's never going to take you seriously. He's sussed you out, Milly, otherwise you'd have told him to fuck off, right?'

She nodded.

'So why should he have any confidence in you? You've got to scare him. Make him sit up. And if he rates you, he'll wear it, like he does with the others, and if he doesn't, well, at least you'll know, and you might as well sack him anyway.'

He was on a roll now.

'Otherwise you'll just carry on in limbo for ever. Knowing nothing and going nowhere.' Jonson had smashed the hammer down again on a nail that was already flush to the wood. He slid his mobile phone over to her. 'And if you don't, I will.'

'You wouldn't!'

'Try me. I'd go round and see him. Then he'd read it.'

Milly took up the phone – and the challenge. She punched in the number and looked at Jonson with her thumb on the green button.

'Give him hell,' urged Jonson.

'Hello, Lyal Roberts, please.'

Jonson punched his fist into his free hand. 'Give him some shit.'

She told him she would.

'Muriel, it's Juliet again. May I speak with Lyal?'

Jonson nodded encouragingly.

Milly held the phone away from her head and mouthed a solo expletive. Jonson wondered what the woman had said to her.

'Okay,' she said into the phone. 'Muriel, could you do me a great favour . . . ?'

'Okay. I've been trying to get hold of Lyal for over five weeks now, and I'd really like to talk to him about my script. Would you mind personally giving Lyal a new copy of the script today and please tell him that I'll be calling—'

Jonson kicked her under the table, shook his head vigorously and pointed from his eyes to hers.

'Scrub that, Muriel. Could I please make an appointment now to come and see Lyal next week to discuss it?'

Jonson beamed and stuck up his thumb.

'That's fine, Muriel. Thank you.' She hit the red button, and blew out her cheeks. 'Three o'clock on Friday afternoon,' she said.

Jonson clapped. 'Well, Milly, if that was you giving them shit, then I wish you were my boss,' he teased her.

She didn't mind his leg-pulling. What she'd just done was a big departure for her and for the first time that day she felt a sense of value again. The cloud was gone.

'Jonson, you're a bloody godsend. I'm so glad you stopped by.'

'I've just had another idea.'

'Oh?'

'If he doesn't like it, I'll be your agent,' he joked.

Milly laughed. 'Yeah, right. I think I'll stick with Lyal.'

'In my hands, you never know what I could do,' he said, rubbing them together.

'The last time it was in your hands, you bloody lost it.'

'You just won't let that go, will you,' he said, as both of them laughed.

Of the two hundred million households in the United States only three, remarkably, were Millhouse residences. The ever positive but increasingly desperate Mitch Carmichael decided that this was great news. 'Good job her name wasn't Kennedy, eh?' he said to his team. He drew a blank with the first two, then stared at the last number on the list. He dialled, and the number began to ring. It rang and rang while Mitch idly discussed other strategies with his team.

A man lay in his bath as his phone rang.

He'd decided to let it go but the damn thing just kept on ringing. It rang way beyond the point where the caller could be allowing for a really big house or a lost cordless.

It had to be an emergency, and so he launched himself out of the bath and lunged for the phone. Now he needed to answer it more than anything in the world. If he missed it he was going to have to kill someone, probably the person on the other end.

'Yeah,' he bellowed venomously into the phone.

Mitch had forgotten it was ringing and was startled.

'Sorry. Hello, Mr Millhouse,' Mitch said, full of expectation.

'Don't tell me you're sellin' something, buddy.'

'Er, no.'

'Well, what, then?'

'May I speak with Juliet, please?'

'Hang on,' the man said gruffly. 'Juliet . . . Phone call.'

Mitch now knew what it felt like to have a heart attack. He'd been expecting the man to say, 'Who?' then crash the receiver down. He looked up at his team, who were trying to determine what was afoot.

'Who is it?' the man barked at Mitch. 'She's a pain in the ass. She doesn't take calls from just anyone.'

As far as Mitch was concerned she was measuring up perfectly to the genius-recluse profile they'd fixed on.

'My name is . . .'

'Oh, yeah. Hang on.'

The receiver thumped on to a table or similar. 'Juliet it's that guy. Next time, answer the goddamn phone, why don't ya?'

'Mitch. Is it her?' Scott hissed.

'I don't know. It's a Juliet Millhouse, though.' He could hardly get the words out.

The receiver was picked up. 'Hello?'

Mitch was amazed by how young she sounded. Almost childlike. 'Juliet? Juliet Millhouse?'

'You took your time calling,' the girl said.

'Well, you didn't give me much to go on.'

'Did you get my note?' she asked.

'What note?'

'This is Ed Davis, right?'

'No.'

'You're not calling about the prom?'

Mitch was devastated. First, this wasn't Juliet Millhouse the writer, and second, he was about to break a schoolgirl's heart. 'No,' he said, and she hung up.

'Fuck,' Scott said. 'I thought that was it.'

'Me too. Another dead-end, huh? Anyone got any suggestions?' Mitch asked. No one had. 'Well, I have. Scott. I need a real big favour from you.'

'Anything, man, you know that.'

'Would you take Dolores out and try to get some information out of her?'

'You're serious!'

Mitch nodded that he was.

'No fucking way, man.'

'But you said you'd do anything.'

'But take Dolores out? Shit, Mitch, I've got to live in this town. Where would I take her?'

'I don't know. To the movies or something.'

'No way. What if she gets the wrong idea? I'd have to kill myself.'

'Okay, okay. I only asked because I'm desperate.'

'Well, that's perfect then – *you* take her out.'

'Oh, come on, be serious,' Mitch said.

'How come I could do it but not you? What is it? You're out of her league, right, and she's more of a match for me?'

'Don't be stupid.'

Scott had always been insecure about the way he looked, and the fact that his wife had run off with a hot-dog vendor at the Laker Stadium hadn't helped.

'So you're not going to do it, then?'

'Damn right I'm not.'

'Karl?' Mitch asked.

'I'd love to help but I think it would be even more suspicious if I asked her out, don't you?' Karl was gay.

'So we're back to square one.'

Josie appeared at the door, and he beckoned her in.

'Mitch, your ex-wife called. Wants to meet with you urgently.'

This wasn't good news. Joely was only calling because she'd heard about his new-found value. Word was out. Spread through Hollywood like the Ebola virus at a Woodstock reunion.

'And I've had calls from casting agents requesting the script,' Josie went on. 'Actors' and directors' agents too – and Ang Lee's office has been on. They want to set up a meeting. Legal have been on saying that they have no record of this option agreement and—'

Mitch raised his hand. 'Whoa. Don't tell me, lemme guess. Elvis has been found and he wants to star in it.'

But Josie hadn't finished. 'And Dolores called, twice. About the meeting with Juliet. I scheduled it for next Wednesday.'

'Way ta go.'

'Oh, come on, Mitch, what else could I do? She was pissed that you hadn't already put it in.'

Mitch stood up, frustrated. 'I now have exactly one week to find this woman. Someone wrote that script, and we have to find her.'

'Perhaps we're looking in the wrong place,' Josie blurted out, trying to redeem herself after being the bearer of such bad news.

Mitch gestured for her to go on.

'So far we've limited our search to literary America,' she said.

Her theory was that the whole thing was a wind-up.

'It's all so cryptic, almost like a joke. The name of the film! Is that its name or is it just a working title? And her name, "Millhouse". Not a particularly common American name, as we've found out.'

Mitch's mind began to race. Maybe Millhouse was English. The name had a certain Englishness about it. And Willenheim had recently been to England. Josie was about to blow her cover with her hoax theory when Mitch stepped in, both saving her and making her the hero of the hour.

'She's English,' he said resolutely.

'Exactly,' Josie agreed.

'Josie, you're a genius.' He kissed her forehead. 'Now we do in England the same as we've done here. Start with the literary agencies.'

CHAPTER NINE

Lyal was having dinner with a beautiful woman of almost half his age. Since he had made the date, he'd spent most of his energy trying to convince himself that his intentions for the evening were honourable. And if they did fall into bed and make love all night, it would be a mistake and not his fault. In his ten-year marriage, he had never been unfaithful to his wife, for which he thought his wife should be enormously grateful. Truth was, he'd never had the opportunity.

Amber was the press secretary of the Albery Theatre, home to Dylan Walsh's new hit play. Lyal hadn't seen her since the play had opened, but he'd conspired to talk to her frequently on the phone. He had even given her the number of his direct line to bypass Muriel. Rave notices abounded, and the play had sold out, so Amber's work was complete, which was why Lyal had been so nervous in organising this dinner. Was he signalling his intent too obviously? He bloody well hoped so.

They had a secluded table at Bibendum in Chelsea, and so far all was going according to plan.

'Do you like being an agent?' she asked.

'Well, it's a tough job, but someone's gotta do it.'

Amber laughed at his little joke, and he refilled her glass with Chablis. Plenty more where that came from.

'But seriously though, yeah I do. My clients are important to me and I really look to protect them.'

'Dylan says you're one of the most successful agents in the country.'

Nice one, Dylan. Boy, was she up for it! He'd told his wife he was going to watch the Arsenal game, and he wondered whether she'd know it was a league match, which wouldn't have extra time. 'Well, an agent is only as good as his list, but my list is as good as anybody's so, yes, I guess I am.' His erection now took a firm hold on proceedings; he fervently hoped he would be needing it later on.

'It must be very glamorous. Premières and opening nights.'

'Yes – but, it's not all glamour. There's a lot of hard work too. But once that's done, then yes I like to play.'

'With all the people you must meet, I'm surprised your wife ever lets you out.'

How did she know I was married? Probably trying to find out, the little minx. He thought it best neither to confirm nor deny it.

'So, tell me,' she said, 'what's the best part of your job?'

'Well . . .' he pretended to be deep in thought '. . . this might sound a little sentimental but although I enjoy looking after the likes of Dylan, Mark Devlin and Shaun O'Leary . . .' he dropped in the last two names casually so that there could be no doubt about his status '. . . I love nurturing new talent.'

'How noble.'

'You see, Amber . . .' That's good. Use her name. That was one of *GQ*'s tips of this month for coaxing the panties down. '. . . I get a hell of a kick out of helping new young writers. It's lonely out there on your own with just a PC for company. And, of course, when they make it, it's them that make *me* successful. I never forget that. A good agent is an agent without an ego.'

'Do you think Dylan's play could transfer to Broadway?'

Lyal laughed. 'Do I? It's a certainty. I'll sell the film rights too.'

'Really?' She sounded excited.

'It's in the bag.'

'Wow! Have you told him?'

Lyal hadn't spoken with Dylan all week. The ungrateful shit hadn't returned any of his calls. The worm had turned. 'No. We've been playing telephone tennis all week, but we've got a meeting pencilled for next Thursday,' he lied.

'Oh, I hope you haven't.'

'Huh?' Lyal asked.

'He hasn't told you yet?'

A shaft of panic took hold. Told me what? 'Told me what?'

'Dylan and I are going to the Maldives.'

'You and Dylan?' he spluttered.

'We're going out together. Isn't it great?'

His erection collapsed. He was speechless, furious – with himself for misreading Amber so badly and with Dylan. And what would Dylan think of his agent trying to shag his new squeeze? God, how he *loathed* the bastard.

'I didn't know Dylan and Claire had split up,' he said

sanctimoniously. He saw no hypocrisy whatsoever in his deciding to veer off the motorway heading for 'Adultery' at the junction signposted 'Moral High Ground'. Poor old Claire, he thought, as jealousy totally consumed him. The waiter placed in front of them the most beautifully presented desserts. The central focus was two glazed and sweetened limes on top of mint crème fraîche, with a kiwi-and-gooseberry garnish and enormous fresh pistachio nuts around half the circumference of the plate. It was a green delight, and yet not anything like as green as Lyal.

Milly knocked on her old front door. She hadn't visited her parents for nearly three weeks. Her dad seemed tired to her when he opened the door. In recent years he'd aged dramatically. 'Glad you could come over, Juliet. You know we always love to see you,' he said quietly.

Milly went through into the all-beige sitting room and kissed her mum. 'You're looking well, Mum,' she said, and meant it.

'Thank you, dear. I wish I could say the same for you.'

Milly sighed, remembering why visiting her parents was becoming difficult. Her mother normally waited until halfway through the evening to launch into her diatribe about how Milly really should think about a husband. Tonight, though, she was straight out of the blocks. It must have been on her mind.

'You look lonely, Juliet. Any boyfriends on—'

'Let's not go through this again, Margaret,' her dad said. 'She's only just walked in.'

'There must be some very nice unmarried men at your

work,' Margaret went on, as though he hadn't spoken.

'Mum, this is ridiculous. Why can't you believe I don't want a man at the moment?'

Her mum's eyes widened. 'And what does that mean exactly?'

Milly knew exactly what *she* meant. Magazines were currently awash with articles about all women having lesbian tendencies and an increasing proportion of women willing to explore them. 'No, Mum, it doesn't mean that at all. We've been through this already. And I'm not getting married and having kids just for your sake. If it happens, that's great. I'd love it. But if it doesn't, that's fine too.'

Milly hoped that might be the end of this particular subject.

'Well, you might not be in a hurry, but your ovaries . . .'

Milly groaned as she continued being savaged by a blunt instrument. Her mother appeared to be in a particularly combative mood, which called for her ultimate weapon. 'Anyway, most of the men at work are gay.'

'Oh, God save us. Well, you don't want to get involved with any of that lot!'

'How's the writing coming along, Juliet?' her dad asked, out of genuine interest, but also to quell his wife.

'Erm, not bad, Dad, thanks.'

'Has that chap of yours read it yet?' It was apparent from her reaction that he hadn't. 'Perhaps he's busy, eh. I'm sure he'll get to it.'

Milly smiled at him fondly. She always felt guilty that she'd never shown her work to her parents, but she knew that they wouldn't like it.

'Have you thought about writing children's books, dear?' her mother asked.

'No,' Milly answered firmly. 'Mum, I don't want to write kids' books.'

'Don't knock it, dear. Look at Enid Blyton. Didn't do her any harm.'

'What was that film you saw the other day, darling? The one you liked so much,' her dad intervened again.

'Oh yes, it was very funny. Now, what was it called?' her mother said.

'Was it at the cinema?' Milly asked.

'No, it was on television. I watched it down here. Howard, do you remember? You wanted to watch that silly war thing so you had to go upstairs to the portable . . . Oh, what was it called?'

'What was it about, Mum?'

'Oh, it was very funny.'

'Who was in it?'

'That nice American girl. The one who's in everything.'

'Renee Zellweger.'

'Who? No. This girl's famous. She cried at the Oscars, bless her, and went on about loving her parents.'

The penny dropped. Actually, she'd gone on about loving her dad.

'Gwyneth Paltrow.'

'That's the one.'

Milly had an idea that *Sliding Doors*, a film she hadn't enjoyed at all and whose success she was at a loss to understand, had been on television the other night.

'Oh, it doesn't matter, Mum. Dad, how's the allotment?' she asked, shifting the subject on to literally much safer ground.

'Oh, not bad. Could do with a bit of sunshine, but the marrows are . . .'

'*Sliding Doors*,' her mother shrieked. 'Yes, it's all about . . .'

Milly sighed and her dad went quiet, waiting for his chance to talk about his allotment, and in particular about his beloved marrows. Despite the fact that no one in the world actually likes marrows, they are still grown with passion by amateur gardeners because of their enormously satisfying size. Big, burgeoning green phalluses, lying there for everyone to see. Milly smiled as she remembered her dad every summer proudly lugging home his crop which, via the dinner table, inevitably ended up in the bin. Even their old Labrador drew the line at marrows, and she'd once eaten the entire contents of a full nappy. For young men, it's their tackle, and for old men it's their marrows.

'What are you smiling at, Juliet?' her dad asked wryly, although he had a good idea why.

'I was just thinking about your . . .'

'Come on, spit it out,' her mother said, unaware of her appropriate turn of phrase.

'Spit them out,' Milly barely managed. 'I was thinking about Dad's marrows.'

Her dad smiled and her mother suddenly became very animated.

'He's growing the wretched things again this year. Howard, why can't you grow things we like?'

'I try. I'm doing sprouts this year.' He laughed.

His attempts at the more palatable vegetables were always a disaster. His cabbages were like sprouts and his runner beans always looked knackered, like the stragglers in the London marathon.

'I've already got one this big, Juliet,' he said, joining in the fun, holding out his hands like a fisherman exaggerating his catch.

'Wow. Just what I need, eh, Mum?'

Her mother was a desperate prude, but in this instance even she allowed herself to see the funny side, and all three of them shrieked with laughter. It had taken twenty years or so to find a good use for her dad's blasted marrows – to give them all a good laugh. Twenty sodding years of pushing them around a plate, but it had been worth it.

Mitch discovered quickly that making speculative calls to literary agents was a slow process. First of all, there were the pleasantries, then the 'what's new' interlude, which eventually made way for the reason for the call in the first place. No one represented a Juliet Millhouse, but they were all keen to discuss their other clients and any new scripts they might have penned. Some were a little more hopeful than that. 'I've got a Juliet Sharp. Will she do?'

Wearily he punched in another number.

'Good morning. ILM.'

'Hello. Lyal Roberts's office, please.'

The call was patched through.

'Hello, Lyal Roberts's office.'

'Yeah, hi. It's Mitch Carmichael here from Pacific Studios. Could I speak with Lyal, please?'

'One moment.'

Lyal was still nursing his injured pride from the previous evening. He stared at his ringing telephone and glanced up at Muriel, who had just appeared at his door. 'Mitch Carmichael,' she mouthed.

Mitch? Lyal thought. Haven't spoken to him for a while. Let's hope this is good news.

'Mitch, hi,' Lyal said into the phone. 'How's it going?'

'Lyal, I'm in a bit of a rush. You don't happen to look after a writer called Juliet Millhouse, do you?'

Lyal didn't need to think. The one thing he did know was his client list. 'Nope,' he said.

Mitch gave him a moment, expecting the offers of other clients and other hot scripts, but Lyal wasn't forth-coming.

'Thanks, Lyal.'

'Okay.'

A cruel succession of events had just conspired against Mitch, Lyal and, most importantly, Milly. Had Mitch asked Muriel that question, he might have received a different answer. A divorcee herself, Muriel had advised Milly not to revert to her maiden name of Millhouse for her writing but to continue as Juliet Phillips. It was also sheer bad luck that Milly, in a fit of pique, had signed the fated script with her maiden name, Millhouse – four years on and Elliot was still causing her hurt.

*   *   *

Claudia was having breakfast with Monty Ross and she didn't want anyone to see her. That would change, of course, if this meeting went according to plan. Monty Ross was second-in-command at Columbia Pictures, with an illustrious movie career behind him. He was not quite a Willenheim but he was a big player. He smiled at her, revealing his brilliant set of square white teeth. They looked odd in his old head – he had to be at least seventy-five. Sadly, her daddy wasn't the dental miracle worker responsible but Claudia felt confident that she could make her own breaks from now on anyway.

'So, Claudia, what is it that you have for me?' he asked, with a lewd intonation. He was well known for enjoying the company of beautiful women.

'We've got a picture that Willenheim has gone nuts about.' Claudia knew there was no love lost between Ross and Willenheim – they'd crossed swords twenty years ago when they'd worked together at MGM.

Ross knew that the fact that she even mentioned the picture must mean that it was potentially still available. Otherwise what would be the point – so that he should look out for it at the theatres?

'Is is still available? What's it called? Who's producing?' Monty was now very businesslike.

'That's just it. No one seems to know anything about it. I'm working in Development, right? None of us have ever heard of the script, or the writer.'

'What the hell's going on over there?'

'The way I figure it is this. Somehow Willenheim has seen this script, but we don't own it. And my colleagues are busting their asses trying to find it.'

Monty stroked his saggy neck, which was scheduled to be tightened a week on Friday. 'What about contracts?' he asked.

'I've checked with Legal and they don't have any record of an option agreement.' Claudia sensed that she was about to prevail.

'So, what do you want to do, then?'

The fish was hooked and now she had to be brave. 'That depends on what it's worth to your studio.'

He smiled slowly. 'I'm sure I could clear a nice corner office for you at Columbia.'

In many ways, Claudia knew, this would be a sideways step, but it would put her at the foot of a big ladder. He held out his hand, which she took. If she really wanted to climb this ladder, she'd have to get used to handling him.

None of the usual literary routes in England had come through with anything for Mitch, but Josie had found eight Millhouses in England, two of whom were ex-directory. He looked at the list, then dialled the first number.

'Hello,' a clipped female voice answered.

'Good morning, ma'am. My name is Mitch Carmichael, and I'm looking for a Juliet Millhouse.'

'Who?'

Mitch's eyes rolled and he cut the connection. 'Next.' He dialled another number.

A new line, a new number and a new ringing tone filled his office.

''Allo.' It was a gruff voice this time.

'Is that the Millhouse home?' Mitch asked mechanically, without any real hope.

'Yeah. Wot about it?'

'I'm looking for a Juliet Millhouse.'

''Oo are you?'

He looked at his team. He didn't want to get too excited yet.

'Is Juliet there? Juliet Millhouse?'

'No. She's at work. 'Oo's this?'

Mitch had to battle with all his emotions, which were urging him to let rip. 'Juliet Millhouse is at work?' he asked, needing confirmation.

'Ah just said that, didn't Ah. 'Oo are you?'

'My name is Mitch Carmichael, and I'm calling from Pacific Studios in Los Angeles.'

'Wot d'you want wiv 'er?'

'Er, I think I have one of her film scripts,' Mitch said.

'She ain't said nuffin' to me about a film. She normally just writes stories.'

Mitch punched the air, and his team held their breath. 'It's very important that I speak with her,' he said. 'Could I call her at work?'

'Do wot you want, mate. Don't bovver me.'

'Can I have the number?'

''Ang on.' There was a long pause. 'Right, 'ere you are.' And he disclosed a number.

Mitch hung up and screamed into his hands. 'It *must* be her! The boyfriend didn't even know about the script.'

'Which is exactly what we thought she'd be like,' Scott said.

'Exactly. Secretive.'

'Weird,' Josie added.

Mitch collected himself and dialled the number.

'Hello, Embassy Publishing,' a bright woman said. A publisher's!

'Could I speak to Juliet Millhouse, please?'

'We have a Julie Millhouse.'

'That's the one!'

'Putting you through.'

''Allo.' A brusque Cockney accent shattered the calm.

'Juliet?' Mitch asked, this time full of passion and hope.

'Yeah. 'Oo's this?'

'You don't know me. My name is Mitch Carmichael. I'm calling about your film script.'

Silence.

'Yeah. Wot about it?' she said suspiciously, suspecting it was a friend winding her up.

'I'd like to buy it. Well, I'd like to meet with . . .'

''Ow jew get 'old of it? 'Oo are you again?'

'Mitch Carmichael. Head of Development at Pacific Studios in Los Angeles.'

'Oh, yeah, right. Fuck off.' The line went dead.

Mitch looked up at his team. He pushed his hands through his hair. 'She's playing hardball.' He hit a button on his console. 'Nikki, would you get me the first flight to London this afternoon? The usual hotel is fine.'

CHAPTER TEN

The Juliet Millhouse that Mitch had found was better known to her readers as Joo-Leigh. She had worked for Embassy Publishing for the past five years following a spell on various local papers. Embassy currently had four publications: *Big Jugs*, *Real Birds*, *Shaven Ravens* and *Office Hussies*. They occupied the lowest possible end of the porn market and their proud owner, Grant Austin, had signalled his intent to add some other more classy skin titles to his range and, furthermore, to branch into the pornographic film business. He was truly a man of vision, and Joo-Leigh was central to his plans.

''Ere, Joo, wot d'jew fink of 'er?' Ray, the picture editor, asked, and handed over a pile of photographs sent in by an amateur hopeful.

Julie glanced at the top picture. 'Fuckin' 'ell, Ray, you can't put 'er in.'

'Why?'

'Ruff as fuckin' dogs, mate.'

'So?' Ray said. 'That's wot they want, innit?'

Julie looked at another picture. 'Poor old cow. If ma tits were that saggy, Ah wouldn't 'ave 'em pierced, Ah can tell ya.'

The woman in question was in her fifties, no doubt a great-grandmother, with stretch marks and cellulite.

She was a pathetic sight, and looked as if she could really use the thirty-five pounds she'd receive if she got published.

It was Julie's job to fill the magazines with stories of sexual debauchery, as many as eight each month. The current edition of *Real Birds* had a sports theme, and Joo-Leigh was halfway through writing a piece on a rugby changing room.

She would have turned straight round and left, but something held her gaze. It was an array of wonderful cocks on equally wonderful bodies. She counted four, and from that deduced that there must have been four men in the room. She hadn't looked at any of their faces. She wanted to, but she couldn't. She couldn't take her eyes off their wonderful cocks. She wanted them all, and it was becoming increasingly obvious that they wanted her. It was as if they were speaking to each other, although no words were uttered. They weren't needed!

She put her bag down, and loosened her blouse as the first man arrived. It was now fully erect and, needless to say, it was fucking massive!

Grant gave each story his personal seal of approval. He read them all in one batch, and usually granted them the highest honour that a porn writer could receive. 'Fantastic, Joo-Leigh. That one about the pole-vaulter . . .'

'Ar, fanks, Grant.'

While Julie was glad that each month she helped possibly thousands of men, she couldn't really be proud of her work. It wasn't something she could ever envisage telling her grandchildren about. For some time now, she'd felt that she had so much more to offer creatively, which was why she was desperate to get into pornographic films. That was where the money and the respect were, and on this Grant was right behind her. He'd read her film scripts and promised he'd get them made.

Milly was famous for her punctuality, so it was unusual to see her flying through the front entrance at 7.30, which made her fifteen minutes late. She didn't have an excuse and wouldn't need one, unless Mr Mahmood was on the prowl. When her alarm had woken her this morning at six o'clock, she was still exhausted from having been up until late writing her diary and had fallen asleep again. She raced into the back office, took off her coat and flew back behind the desk, where Lucas was fielding an enquiry from an irascible old lady. Eventually he calmed her down, sorted her out, then helped her across the lobby to the door for Samson to find her a taxi.

Milly's mobile phone rang and, foolishly, she allowed herself to get excited. Sadly it didn't say 'Lyal' in the window and crossly she hit the busy button, lost her grip on the phone and watched it smash to the ground. Of course, Sod's law prevailed and it managed to scurry under a filing cabinet. An exasperated Milly was lying flat out, blindly fumbling for it, when the reception bell pinged loudly. It wasn't a gentle 'when you're ready' ping. This was a loud, urgent ring, and Milly, phone in hand, instantly leapt to her feet.

'Oh God, it's you!' she said, trying to stop the words

as they fell out of her mouth. She had forgotten that Mr Mitch Carmichael was due this morning.

Mitch had stayed in hotels the world over but had never been greeted by 'Oh God, it's you' before. He'd also expected someone to appear from the back office and not directly up from the floor.

'I'm sorry,' Milly said, aghast.

He shrugged.

'No. Please. I am so sorry.' She wished she could start again. She'd wanted to make a lasting impression on the man this time but not this one. 'I just didn't expect to see you there, that's all.'

He looked at her oddly, then smiled and said, 'Look, please, don't worry about it.'

'No. But what I meant was . . .'

'In any case, I don't know why you should be so surprised. This is Reception and I do have a reservation.'

'I know you do, Mr Carmichael. I checked ahead to see if you might be staying again.' *Oh God, how am I going to explain that I knew his name?*

'I'm impressed you remembered my name.'

'Well, it hasn't been so long since you were last here. And we don't get many . . . erm . . .' She tailed off, feeling ridiculous: she was behaving like a starstruck schoolgirl. She pulled herself together. 'So!' she said emphatically, hoping to draw a line under the preceding cock-up, 'welcome back to the Shelton Tower, Park Lane, Mr Carmichael. I do hope you enjoy your stay.'

'So do I.'

Milly was furious with herself. Her mates had spent a considerable amount of time on Sunday afternoon making a case for her pitching *Untitled* to him and she had a copy of the script in her bag, ready for him. She couldn't very well give it to him now, though. Her opening salvo had shattered any self-confidence she might have had earlier. Anyway, he looked tired after his long flight.

Do whatever you can to get your script into the decision-maker's hands.

She was terrified, but she didn't know what she feared the most: rejection, or facing the wrath of Georgina.

She busied herself with processing his room allocation while her mind raced back and forth. Time was running out. He was drumming his fingers on the marble desk. She couldn't help noticing the absence of a wedding band, and wanted to study his boyish features, but he noticed every time she tried to look at him. There were six messages for him to call his office in LA. He was obviously an important man.

'Here we are, Mr Carmichael. You have several messages. You're in Room six one nine, on the sixth floor. Do you have any luggage?'

Mitch held up his smallish overnight bag. His reservation was open ended but clearly he wasn't intending to stay long. Two nights, three tops. *So now is the time, Milly.* She could see Jonson's face imploring her, 'Strike while the iron's hot.' She clenched her fists. 'If you take the lift to the sixth floor, Room six one nine is to your left.'

Come on, Milly. Seize the moment. Seize it!

'Thank you,' he said, and bent down to retrieve his bag.

She took the plunge. 'You're in movies, aren't you?' she blurted out.

'Haven't we done this before?' he said.

'Yes . . . but . . . erm . . . er.' Not exactly impressive use of the great English language from someone just about to announce themselves as a writer. Who do you write for? Tarzan!

'I've written a script, which—'

Carmichael held up his free hand. 'Please. I don't mean to be rude, but you have to understand, practically everyone I've ever met has written a script.'

She couldn't speak – she was bitterly hurt.

He looked at her name badge. 'Milly, if I read every script that was pitched to me, I wouldn't get a chance to eat. So, thank you but no thank you. Do you have an agent?'

'Yes.'

'It's his job to get it to me.'

Fleetingly she wondered whether it might be worth explaining her current situation, but decided that that would be even more embarrassing. In any case, he was walking away.

'I've written a script, which . . .' That was as far as she'd got. She'd lasted all of five paltry words. She felt she had to do something positive – anything to salvage some self-esteem. She took out her mobile and aggressively hit Lyal's pre-programmed number. Tears stood in her eyes, but not tears of sorrow: they were tears of anger.

'Muriel, it's Juliet . . . No. I don't want to speak to him . . . It's about the meeting. It's still on, right? For Friday . . . Good. So he'll have read it then? . . . Right. 'Bye.'

*   *   *

By the time Mitch had got to his room he had read and digested all his messages: three from Scott, two from Josie and, most worryingly, one from Dolores.

First he called Scott's mobile – it was the only way to get hold of him as it was the middle of the night in LA.

'Scott. Mitch.'

'Oh, man. How're ya doing? You met her yet?'

'No. Flight was delayed. So, what's up? Everyone's been calling me.'

'Good job you ain't here, buddy. Shit's hit the fan.'

'Go on.' Mitch sat down on his enormous bed.

'Willenheim gets a call from his lawyer. Apparently, Columbia know about the script and are searching for it too.'

'Shit.' But he wasn't altogether surprised. News like this couldn't be contained for long in Hollywood. Sharks can smell a drop of blood up to two miles away, and he'd been haemorrhaging down Hollywood Boulevard.

'How did they find out?' he asked, reflexively.

'No one knows. But Claudia resigned today.'

Mitch wished he hadn't asked.

'Willenheim's gone totally nuts. Sacked one of his assistants and chewed off Dolores. She's real pissed at ya.'

'She's called,' he said.

'You *bet* she has. Poor old Josie was right in the firing line when the news broke on the internal mail. Then word came down that Willenheim was on his way to our floor.'

'*What?*' Mitch could hardly believe his ears. Scott might as well have said that Willenheim had taken the bus to work.

'Yes. And Josie was the only one there, and she had a panic attack.'

'How do you mean?'

'Shit Mitch. You know, she panics. Loses it, freaks out. What would you do? Willenheim is on his way down to our floor remember. She was either getting iced or ratting you out.'

Mitch didn't respond, just blew his cheeks out.

'She's smart. She manages to pass it off as an epileptic fit. Paramedics were called and everything. She's quite the little actress. They carried her out stiff as a board, but they used a stretcher anyway.'

'Where is she now?'

Scott laughed. 'Get this. She's still in hospital man, having all kinds of tests. I saw her earlier today, she is so pissed at you.'

'Isn't everyone? Tell her thank you, and that I'll make it up to her, I promise.' He was touched by his team's loyalty, but he also felt terribly guilty for compromising them all so badly. Just like in the movies, he had survived. He'd got out just in time, just ahead of the building exploding, but unlike the hero, he'd left all his team sitting comfortably at their desks wondering what they were going to have for lunch.

'It'll all be worth it, Scott. I'm about to call Juliet now,' Mitch added, 'but I need to get rid of this heat. You got Dolores' home number?'

'You *serious*?'

'Sure.'

It was now a do-or-die situation. His back was against the wall, and he had nothing to lose. Indeed any number of cliches, suddenly seemed particularly apt at this time. But he had found his writer and, with the kind of money that he was going to throw at her, soon he'd have her signature on a contract. He was so confident of this that he was going to call Dolores in the middle of the night. He dialled her number. He felt calm – oddly, he was even looking forward to talking to her.

'What?' Dolores bellowed into the phone.

'Dolores, it's Mitch,' he sang. 'I got a message you needed to speak with me urgently.'

'Do you know what freaking time it is? And do you have any idea how much shit you're in?'

'I hear you got chewed off today. I'm sorry about that.'

'Carmichael. You listen to me—'

'No. How about you listen to me?' He wished he'd thought to record this conversation because no one back in the office would believe him otherwise. 'While you're asleep, I'm in London, England, conducting a sensitive development meeting with one of the most fragile and brilliant writers of her generation. Now, what I don't need is to be aggravated and harassed by your office about my whereabouts, and I do not want lawyers dispatched from LA because I'm sure what none of us wants is for this young woman to be frightened off. Do you understand me?'

'Mr Willenheim said—'

'Hey, Dolores, do you know what? Why don't *I* worry about Mr Willenheim for the moment, huh? My job is to work for him, to develop movies, and that is exactly what I'm doing here.' Mitch had surprised himself with his eloquence, and it fuelled his confidence for his most important play. 'You can tell Mr Willenheim all this tomorrow morning, or I'll call him right now.'

'No,' Dolores said – she even sounded as if she was about to say 'please', a word most people thought she'd never bothered to learn.

'I'm doing my job and I've got nothing to hide and if he wants to speak to me that's fine. Just gimme his direct number, and I'll call him,' Mitch said, growing in stature with every word.

'No, no, I'll speak to him.'

'You sure, now?'

'Yes,' she hissed.

'Tell him he can call me any time. But if I start seeing lawyers from the States over here, or anyone else for that matter, it'll be down to them if my writer gets cold feet.'

Mitch hung up, feeling charged and invigorated. He'd never asserted himself like that before and it felt good. He now understood why Willenheim was ritually horrible to everyone. With such excitement, he was busting to pee. He entered his *en suite* bathroom. He lifted the wooden seat and there staring up at him were the remains of the room's previous occupant. Not even a floater could dent his mood. He took aim and bombarded it to smithereens.

Milly had drunk a litre bottle of Highland Spring but still hadn't quenched her thirst. Georgina had phoned to see how it had gone and had assured her that she'd done the right thing. Well, Georgina was wrong. Milly felt utterly dejected and wished she'd never tried to get into the movie business in the first place. The film industry was clearly for individuals who had been born with hides rather than skins, people who used dung and mud as moisturiser, while Milly was pussying around in herbal baths.

Mr Mahmood swooped into Reception, as ever back rigid, arms at his sides, legs beating back and forth like pistons. 'Everything okay here, Mill-ee?' he asked as he breezed by, as if he were on a skateboard. It was a rhetorical question, she knew, so she didn't answer.

Suddenly, he came to an abrupt stop, as if his front wheels had hit a pencil, except his momentum didn't send him flying. He'd spotted an esteemed guest in need of some pampering.

'Mr Nakasoto, what a pleasure to have you back at our hotel.' Mr Mahmood bowed to greet his Japanese guest. 'And where is your charming wife?'

Mr Nakasoto looked mournful. 'I have lost her,' he said.

Mr Mahmood laughed heartily. 'Well, I should nott worry,' he said. 'She's probably gone straightt through to the lounge.'

Mr Nakasoto looked uncomfortable, and in a flash Mr Mahmood realised his error. 'Oh, my God, what have I said? Mr Nakasoto, I amm so sorry,' he said. It was clear that Mr Nakasoto wanted to forget the *faux pas*, but the hotelier with his head bowed in utter contrition failed to pick up on this. 'What a tragic loss for you. Pliss if there is anything we can do to mek it easier for you at this time . . .'

Mr Nakasoto had now been joined by his new wife or girlfriend. She had been waylaid at the jewellery window in the lobby, no doubt choosing something to wear tonight. She was about half his age, twice his height, blonde, buxom, blue eyed, and nothing like his late Japanese wife. Mr Nakasoto had evidently got over his bereavement, and it occurred to everyone that he might even have had a hand in her death. There was nothing anyone could say. 'Way ta go, Mr Nakasoto' sprang to mind, as did the more simple but equally poignant 'Result'.

'Joo-Leigh!' Grant shouted across the office.

'Wot?' she shouted back. She was in the middle of writing her regular column for *Shaven Ravens*, entitled 'Eager for the Beaver', and was currently mining a rich seam of filth.

'It's that geezer,' Grant yelled.

'Wot fuckin' geezer?'

'You know. That American. The geezer on about your flick.'

Julie looked confused. Grant and all her mates had assured her that they hadn't played any kind of joke on her but she still didn't believe the call had been for real. She picked up the phone. 'You better not be messin' me around.'

'I ain't. I swear,' he protested.

''Allo,' she bellowed.

'Hi, it's Mitch Carmichael from Pacific Studios. We spoke, er, two days ago and we need to meet. Really.'

'Is this a wind-up or wot?' Julie asked.

Mitch didn't understand her question. 'I just want the opportunity to meet you, that's all.'

'You wanna talk about me films.'

'I wanna buy them,' Mitch said.

Julie sniffed. 'You wanna *buy* 'em?'

'Absolutely.'

'Which film jew wanna buy 'cos there's three of 'em. Like in a sequence.'

Mitch's heart raced. A trilogy!

'Well, all of them, then,' he said.

'You ain't takin' the piss?'

'I'm in London now. Ready to meet.'

'Blimey.' Julie still wasn't convinced but she desperately wanted to be. This was exactly the break she needed, the break she *deserved*.

'I'm at the Shelton Tower, Park Lane. Do you know it?'

Julie laughed. 'Not really, but I'm sure Ah can find it.'

'Great! Well, what about now?' Mitch said, and immediately wished he hadn't. First rule of negotiation: never show how interested you are. But then again, the fact that he'd flown six thousand miles after being told to 'fuck off' was proof enough that he was fairly interested.

'Ah can't come now. Ah've got a deadline. 'Ow about Latar?'

'What time?'

'Will you 'ave the money wiv ya?'

What a crude question at such an early stage in the negotiation! But Mitch was going to give her whatever she wanted.

'I won't have all of it with me now. I've got a basic option agreement here, and I'm authorised to write you a cheque for the first fifty. The rest will have to come from the States.'

'Is that the best you can do? Fifty ain't a lot, mate. Not for a film like this.'

Mitch smiled. So she was human after all, just like the rest of us, chasing the green. Like many Americans, Mitch found the English a baffling race. This woman certainly had a very peculiar voice. Whilst it seemed different to Winslet's voice and Paltrow's accent in *Emma*, it was still quintessentially English and frightfully posh, as indeed all English people were.

'Okay, Juliet. Let's not waste each other's time. Let's say two hundred thousand dollars up front, but I can only write out a cheque for fifty today.'

Julie, who currently made twenty-four thousand pounds a year, had assumed he'd meant fifty pounds, not fifty thousand, so she could be excused for nearly passing out. 'Shall I bring 'em wiv me? The scripts?' she asked, quivering.

'Absolutely. I want to see 'em straight away. In fact I'd like to do a read-through with you.'

'What?' She was surprised, because they weren't much of a read: a few scene changes with more grunts and groans than dialogue. 'Well, there ain't much to read. They're more action films, int they?'

'Whatever. We could get together today in my hotel suite. You could take a part and I could take a part, and we'll go through them. I have to tell you, I can't wait. Would you be up for that?'

Now it all made perfect sense to Julie. This guy was just after a shag. He was a loaded septic tank with a weird way of buying fluff. Strictly speaking, she hadn't been paid for sex before, but for the money this bloke was talking, he could do whatever he liked.

'So, four thirty, then,' the American said.

'Awright.'

'Oh, before you go, my boss needs to see them and we're working to a really strict timetable. Do you have them with you?'

'Yeah. On me peecey.'

'What?'

'Me peecey. Me computa.'

'Could you print them off? I'm going to arrange for a courier to pick them up and get them to LA.'

'Fine.'

Joo-Leigh was in a state of near-collapse.

CHAPTER ELEVEN

Jonson sat back in his seat as the plane bound for Los Angeles climbed into the skies over Heathrow. A new chapter in his life had opened and he was flying in more ways than one. His career was really taking off. The catalyst had been the christening, when God must have chosen him for some higher purpose. And as long as that didn't involve him giving all his stuff to the poor, then he felt ready to take up the mantle. This was his second international business trip since that day, but there was no club-class seat this time. Instead, he was holed up at the back of the economy cabin, next to the toilet, with a copy of *Loaded* and an urgent package for a Mr A. Willenheim, Pacific Studios, Los Angeles. The package had come from the Shelton Tower, and Milly had swung him the job, of course – probably as a way of apologising to him for all the grief that she and Georgina had given him for losing her script.

A triumphant but exhausted Mitch was in his luxury hotel suite. For the past eleven days, he hadn't had a moment to himself, and now he faced the luxury of almost a whole day with nothing to do. Having dozed for an hour or so, and having watched the news loop on CNN twice, he turned his attention to the in-room movies. He'd seen them all apart from *Office Frolics* and *Girl Power*. He hadn't watched a pornographic film since his college days and he wondered whether the odd (but equally attractive) receptionist would know if he selected *Office Frolics*. But then he saw the notice: *All films will appear as FILM on your invoice.* Perfect! He entered his room number on his remote control, and the film was beamed in. He'd missed the opening, but was confident he could pick it up. An attractive lady had arrived at an office for an interview and, after some cursory questions, the two adults decided to have sex. She must get the job now, Mitch thought, laughing. It would be criminal if she didn't. Thanks for the blowjob, we'll let you know. Hollywood carried its stresses and strains, but Mitch suddenly felt relieved and privileged to be a part of the real movie business, and he was heartened to know that Juliet's magnificent scripts were currently *en route* to Willenheim.

Julie had to fudge the end of her piece for her 'Eager for the Beaver' column. She was just too excited at the prospect of meeting this crazy American.

Grant agreed that the Yank was probably just after a pork, but he still felt there was a chance he might want her scripts. Either way, he was adamant that he should attend the meeting too, with which Julie had concurred. Given the money involved and the grandiose venue, he had decided that they should arrive in style and had hired a white stretch limo for the journey.

That afternoon London was busy as the hideous air-conditioned monstrosity inched its way down the Strand, burning off a litre of unleaded each yard. Grant and Julie partook freely of the complimentary champagne from the car's fridge.

'This is the fuckin' life, eh, Joo?' Grant said.

'People all starin' at us – look.'

One young man in a baseball cap with baggy jeans crossed in front of the car and glanced at it scornfully.

'Whass up wiv 'im?' Joo-Leigh asked.

''E's fuckin' jealous. Go on, piss off, you, this is as close to a limo as you'll ever get, pal.'

Julie leant back in her seat and took another gulp of her champagne.

'If it's just sex 'e's after, right, you gotta get outta the room, Grant, 'cos Ah can't bang 'im wiv you watchin'.'

'No problem, babes. 'E gets 'is cock out, I'm gone. But 'e starts shovin' it where 'e shouldn't . . . you know, the old lane change . . . you just scream out, 'cos I'll be right outside.'

'Don't worry, Ah will.'

'Anyway, let's 'ope it don't come to that, eh? 'E might want the scripts.'

'What then, though?' Julie asked.

'Then I'm your agent. You just leave it to old Grant here.'

'Why? You done this before, then?'

'No. 'Course I fuckin' 'aven't.'

Milly's mobile phone rang again and she slipped into the back office. She expected it would be Jonson calling from the airport but her heartbeat picked up when she saw 'Lyal' in the display window. She let it ring a few times

while she composed herself. Then she clicked to answer.
'Hello.'

'Hello, Juliet, it's Muriel. How are you?'

'I'm fine . . . You?' Milly sensed that Muriel wasn't
calling with good news.

'The usual . . . busy as ever.'

An awkward silence followed and Milly's dread grew.

'Juliet, I'm sorry . . .'

It was a cancellation call and she didn't need to hear
the rest. Something about a trip to LA, but it didn't matter
to her. She hated Lyal too much to be impressed by that.

'He's terribly sorry. He was looking forward to seeing
you.'

'Is he around? Can I have a word with him?' Milly
asked, her voice a mixture of anger, hurt and self-pity.

'He's had to rush off to a meeting, I'm afraid.'

'Has he read it?'

'I don't know, Juliet. I suspect he has—'

'But he hasn't mentioned it?'

'No.'

'Have *you* read it?'

There was a brief silence. 'No. I'm sorry, I haven't.
Juliet, I know you're disappointed, but Lyal will be in
touch. And I will read it. That I promise you.'

'Thanks, Muriel.'

She ended the call, seething with fury. It was a moment
or two before she could bring herself to return to the desk.
When she opened the office door, she saw a strange-
looking couple waiting for attention. The man was
wearing a gold chain round his neck, earrings in both ears
and a gold tooth, and she looked as if she was in fancy

dress, with a lurid pink boob tube resting on another pink tube which was her stomach. Her navel had most likely been pierced, although it was difficult to tell. She too was a gold fan, and between the two of them they looked like a Ratners shopfront.

'How can I help you?' Milly asked politely.

'We've got a meetin' wiv Mr Carmichael. 'E's stayin' 'ere,' the woman said.

'Mr Mitch Carmichael?' Milly asked, as people do when they don't believe what they've just heard.

'Yeah, that's right.' The man nodded. 'A business meetin'. I'm 'er manager.'

Milly was astounded. Prostitution in hotels is a fact of life, but it was never conducted so openly, and she'd never heard it referred to as a business meeting. Nor had she seen a prostitute quite as unattractive as this woman, with a pimp so insecure he liked to be known as her manager. And why would a man like Mr Carmichael bother with prostitutes? He couldn't possibly be short of female attention.

'He's expecting you, is he?'

'Absolutely.'

Milly dialled his room number.

'Yep.'

'Ah, hello, Mr Carmichael, Reception here'

'Has she arrived?' he asked urgently, cutting Milly off.

'Er, yes—'

'Please hurry her up. I've been waiting all day.'

It was hotel policy to ask for a name but that didn't seem appropriate or necessary in this case. Milly had read many books on Hollywood, about its moguls and

145

their decadent lives, but she was still shocked by how blatant Mitch was, as if it was something to be proud of. She noted from her screen that he had already watched *Office Frolics* and things started to make sense. He was a pervert who liked his bit of rough. All of her self-help books were agreed that *every* situation has a positive side and in this one it was obvious: Mitch Carmichael might be a movie executive but he was a sicko who wouldn't appreciate her writing anyway. It was a good thing that he'd passed up the opportunity to read it. Of that she was certain.

'Mr Carmichael is expecting you. Room six one nine on the sixth floor.'

'Wish me luck, eh?' the woman said.

Milly didn't know how to respond, and barely managed a thumbs-up.

On their way over to the lifts, the man began massaging her shoulders, the way trainers do to boxers before a fight. Wish me luck, a shoulder rub, what was Mr Carmichael going to do to this poor woman?

Moments after they'd knocked Mitch opened his bedroom door and was surprised by the appearance of the couple who stood before him.

'Are you Mitch?' Grant asked.

'Yes. Yes, I am. You must be Juliet and . . . ?'

'Grant.'

The men shook hands, and Mitch beckoned them in. He noticed that Juliet's mouth had dropped open and that she was staring at him as if he was, well, some sort of sex god. Must be overawed, he thought. Gotta put her at her ease – don't want to lose her now.

'Grant, maybe you should leave us,' Juliet said.

She looked at Grant beckoning him to go. 'Maybe me and Mitch should do this alone, eh?'

'No, no,' Mitch assured her, 'why? Three's cool. The more the merrier, right?'

Now it was the man whose mouth had fallen open, although again, Mitch didn't understand why. This couple was certainly odd, but why should that concern him?

'Please, both of you, why don't you take a seat? I have to say, you're not an easy person to find, Juliet.'

'Call me Joo-Leigh.'

'You couldn't have made it more difficult for me, actually. But, hey, we're here now. Can I get you guys a drink? Scotch, beer? I've got pretty much everything here, I think,' Mitch offered.

'Er. Two beers'd be great, fanks,' Grant said.

'Let's make that three.' Mitch busied himself in his minibar, retrieving the only three beers in it.

'So, Mitch, can I ask summink?' Grant said.

'Sure.'

'Wot exactly is goin' down 'ere tonight? 'Cos Joo 'ere, she's up for it. Right. No problems there. And about me getting involved. You sprang that on me there. And it's not summink I've ever considered meself. You know, me and anuvver fellah and that. But Ah might enjoy it. You never know, eh?'

Mitch didn't have a clue what he was talking about. He put their beers on the mahogany table. 'You've brought the scripts, right?'

'Got 'em 'ere,' Juliet announced, and pulled them half out of her case.

They looked thin for film scripts but Mitch wasn't unduly concerned. 'Can I see them?'

Grant put his hand on Julie's bag. 'Of course you can, no problem, but we should take care of the business first. D'you know wot Ah'm sayin'?'

This was a little unorthodox, not least because copies were already on their way to the States. But nothing about this couple or the entire venture had been orthodox so Mitch wasn't surprised. He hadn't pictured his writer looking anything like Julie, though – in fact he thought she looked more like a prostitute with her pimp than a writer with her literary agent. 'Sure, why not?' he said. He produced a four-page option agreement. 'Now, this agreement is for the first movie, which I've called *Untitled*, unless you've come up with a name for it yet. I mean, *Untitled*, is that the title?'

'No! *Body Language*,' Julie said now, excitedly.

Mitch was glad she was relaxing now.

'*Body Language* it is,' he said, and wrote it in. 'These are standard contracts, which I'm sure you've already come across, but obviously you're gonna want to read before you sign.'

'Nah, you're all right, mate,' Grant.interrupted; he grabbed the pen and scribbled.

Mitch was thunderstruck but delighted. Grant had just signed over all rights worldwide. What a relief! Perhaps he was going to make it after all. Mitch Carmichael, Vice-President, Pacific Studios. Then he shook himself and clapped his hands. 'Great!' he said. 'What about some champagne?'

Grant looked awkward. 'Don't wanna be rude, Mitch, but, erm, you know . . . bit premature, int ya?'

'Excuse me?'

'The cheque.'

Mitch hadn't expected to hand it over tonight, but he didn't mind. It was consistent with how everything had been going so far. 'You don't miss a trick,' he joked.

'Fanks.'

Grant almost snatched the cheque out of his hand and studied it, then showed it to Julie, who burst into tears and hugged Grant. 'We've done it, gal. We've fuckin' done it,' he said.

'Oh, Grant, Ah can't believe it.'

Mitch couldn't understand why they were so happy. If it was so important to them, why hadn't she put a telephone number or her agent's details on the bloody script?

'We fort you just wanted to shag 'er,' Grant said.

'*What?*' Mitch screeched.

'Yeah – and me 'n' all,' Grant added.

This was now way beyond weird. Mitch looked at Julie. Why would I want to sleep with *her*? But he didn't want to jeopardise the film deal. He thought it would be best just to move on, as if it hadn't been said. 'So! Shall we get on with the scripts? I've been dying to read this darn thing, I can tell ya, but before I do, I just need to know what it's about. I want to hear the pitch.'

'Wot pitch?' Julie asked.

'The pitch. You sell it to me.'

'We just did,' Grant said.

'I know that, but I want Juliet to talk me through it.'

'Explain it to ya?'

'Exactly.'

'Gotcha,' said Juliet confidently. 'Starts off, right, nice 'ouse, mornin', sunshine. Knock at the door, yeah? Woman comes down the stairs—'

'The star?' Mitch asked.

'Wot?'

'The star of the movie?'

'Yeah, Ah guess she is the star, yeah. I 'adn't fort of her as a star, but I guess she is. She's in almost every scene . . .'

'Wow! Every scene! That's an intense part.'

'Oh, it is. It's intense, awright.'

'Carry on.'

'She's just got outta the shower, yeah, got like a sexy robe on, but she's still a little bit wet . . . yeah?'

'Okay. And she's hot, I take it?' Mitch asked.

'Yeah, well, it's summer, innit?' Grant said.

'Shut up, Grant, 'e don't mean that. 'E means sexy. She opens the front door,' Juliet continued, 'and a mechanic or summink's come to fix summink.'

'Right.' Mitch was wondering where this might be going. Juliet was certainly spending a long time explaining in great detail something which so far seemed fairly inconsequential.

'Cut to the kitchen. She's noshin' 'im off.'

'What?' Mitch asked. An alarm bell screeched in his head.

'She's blowin' 'im. You know, blowjob,' Grant said helpfully, thinking Mitch had misunderstood the term 'noshin''.

'But they've just met,' Mitch protested.

'Exactly. She's a dirty bitch and that's what makes it so sexy.'

Terror took hold in Mitch's mind. He was trying to convince himself that his worst fears were ill founded. Romance in movies was one thing, but a blowjob so early on to a complete stranger was hardly romantic. But there had to be an explanation and as desperate as he was, he looked to Julie to provide one.

'Okay, sure,' Mitch said. 'People like sex in movies, right? Why keep 'em waiting?'

'Exactly, anyway, 'er 'usband's forgotten his lunch, comes 'ome . . .'

Mitch closed his eyes briefly. 'Okay. And what? A fight? A murder?' he asked desperately.

Grant and Julie looked at him blankly.

'No. 'E joins in,' Julie said.

'*What? How?*'

'Up the arse,' Julie said matter-of-factly.

Mitch dropped his head into his hands. His worst fears had come true. This was a porn film. All his hopes were shattered. He was finished. 'Why me?' he whimpered.

'Well, it don't 'ave to be the 'usband, then. It could be anuvva plumba. Maybe she'd phoned two people for quotes. I ain't fussed eaver way.'

Mitch's face was red with a mixture of despair, anxiety and fear. 'This is a porn film, isn't it?' he said, hoping against all hope that they'd say no.

''Course it's a fuckin' porn film, that's wot she writes,' Grant answered.

Mitch began to shake. He had to try to think straight.

Then the full horror of the situation struck him. 'And the movies the courier picked up? They're porn too?'

'Sequels to this one.'

'Oh, my God!'

'Don' you wan' 'em no more?'

'Just go.'

'But you ain't 'eard the others.'

'Just go. Please,' Mitch shouted. 'I don't need to hear any more. I don't buy porn films. Jee-sus, I'm a movie executive. At least, I fucking was . . . Shit!'

He ripped open his bag, took out his cheque book and began to write. 'Here! Take this cheque. It's for you – for your time. I'll need the original one back.'

Grant studied it and reluctantly exchanged it for the first.

'I think five thousand dollars should more than cover your time,' Mitch choked out.

'Fanks, mate.' Juliet was on her way to the door. 'I'll leave me card. You know, in case you change your mind.'

Milly saw the odd couple reappear from the elevator nearly an hour or so after they'd gone up. They looked very pleased with themselves. Whatever it was they had wanted from Mr Carmichael, they'd obviously got it.

'Goodbye, sweetheart,' the woman said to her as they passed.

'Went well, then?' Milly asked, desperate to know more.

'Yeah. Mind you, he's bloody cute – Ah wouldn't 'ave minded shaggin' 'im.'

'You didn't, then?' Milly said, not quite believing what she was asking.

'Nah. 'E didn't want me titties or me movies. He don't want porn. *He wants proper films*,' she said, in her best posh accent.

They turned and walked off towards the lobby entrance. Samson looked at them before they got there. Forty years of experience told him that no money was about to come his way, and so he stayed put.

As soon as they had gone the ever-vigilant Mr Mahmood swooped in. He didn't mind his esteemed guests using the oldest profession in the world, just as long as he knew about it, they were discreet and the whole thing was tastefully executed. The odd couple hadn't met any of these criteria and Mr Mahmood needed answers.

'Mill-ee, who were they, pliss?'

'Difficult to say.'

'Who didd they see?'

'Mr Mitch Carmichael in Room—'

'Six one nine,' he interrupted. 'Film executive with Pacific. Checked in tooday. I know,' he went on. 'Does he look the type?'

'Well, no, not really. But, then, what is the type?'

'Did they come through Benny?'

'I don't think she was a prostitute.'

'Come on, Mill-ee, do I look like a fool?'

'She said something about films.'

Mr Mahmood ignored her. His mind was already made up about the nature of the woman's profession. 'She mustt be the most bloody skint prostitute in Londonne.

And she's not the sort who uses the Shelton Tower, Parkk Lane, I can tell you.' His head swivelled about Reception once more, taking in almost 180 degrees. 'Keep your eye on Mr Carmichael. Make sure he has everything he needs, and if he needs you-know-whatt, make sure he goes through Benny. If word gets out that Benny's been side-lined, we'll have every whoore this side of King's Cross sitting in Receptionne.'

Benny was the hotel's official-unofficial pimp. It was better to have a pimp in control because it meant the hotel was off limits to other girls who might otherwise be clog-ging up the bar in fishnets and too much rouge.

'You all right, Milly?' Lucas asked.

'Did you see that couple who were just in here?'

'Yeah. What was she thinking with the boob tube, man? Anyway, what about 'em?'

'Nothing, really. Just . . .'

Lucas tutted. 'Bloody hell, Milly, anyone'd think you'd just checked in a couple of giant pandas.'

'What do you mean?'

'Now you'll be able to tell your posh mates that you've seen some real working-class people,' he said, in broad Cockney. He goaded Milly regularly for being middle class while exaggerating his own claims to be a working-class boot-boy made good.

'Oh, please. Shut up, Lucas. Like you're some sort of East End villain. I expect your dad ran with the Krays, did he?'

'Working class through and through, me.'

'Yeah, right.'

'Who'd they visit, anyway?'

'Mr Carmichael, the film executive.'

Lucas thought for a second, then leafed through his folder. 'I've got a fax for him. His machine's busted. Nothing getting through.'

'Don't you mean "fru"? Here, give it 'ere. I'll deliver it for ya, gov'nor.'

Mitch had just hung up on Scott. He had things to organise, like cancelling the courier with the scripts, before he could begin to assess the damage. Offering his resignation now didn't seem like a bad idea. At least he was in London, where he was away from the heat in LA. Here he could fob them off a while longer. But what to do now? That was the burning question, and he didn't have any idea where to start. He only had one other lead, the ex-directory listing for a Juliet Millhouse, but he didn't hold out much hope.

The phone rang.

'Hello?'

'What the hell is going on, Carmichael? Dolores says you've lost your mind.'

Willenheim's voice was unmistakable and suddenly six thousand miles felt like six feet.

'Mr Willenheim. I was about to call you, sir.'

'The hell you were! Do you want to tell me what's going on?'

'I'm in London—'

'I know you're in goddamn London. And I've just had a conversation with Jeffrey Reubens at William Morris. Do you know what he tells me?'

Mitch didn't want to know.

'He tells me you haven't got this script and that half of America is looking for this writer. Now, you're gonna tell me that's bullshit, right?'

'Yes, sir, I am.'

'And is it? Don't bullshit me, Carmichael,' the man screamed.

'Yes, sir, it's all bullshit.'

'So explain it to me.'

'Juliet Millhouse is English. She is a sensitive young woman . . .' Mitch wasn't digging a hole for himself, he was drilling with Bruce Willis and the boys in *Armageddon*. '. . . and she has to be handled with kid gloves. That's why it's all been so secret. Any pressure on this girl and she's gone.'

Willenheim was grunting at the other end but clearly listening intently.

'That's why I haven't brought her to the States. LA would freak her out right now. She's a tree-hugger.'

'Carmichael, I don't give a shit how you handle her, but we have the script, right? By that I mean we own the script, right?'

'Yes.'

'Well, then, screw her. Just pay her off and put in a contract writer, for Christ's sake.'

'Not as simple as that, sir.'

'Why?'

'She won't have it. Very protective of her work. Besides, you said it yourself, sir, the script is wonderful. Why ruin it with a contract writer?'

It was a timely piece of thinking on Mitch's part.

'Why haven't Legal got a copy of this contract?' Willenheim bellowed. 'Carmichael, if you've done this independently, you'll never work in movies again, do you understand me?'

'I haven't done that, sir.'

'So why haven't Legal got a fucking contract, then?'

'I don't know. That's their problem, not yours or mine, but I'll send you a copy today. It'll be—'

'Fax it.'

There was a knock at Mitch's door. 'One second, sir.'

Mitch opened the door with the phone still in one hand. Milly was standing there with a fax for him. She needed him to sign for it. He noticed again how pretty she was, by far the nicest thing he'd seen all day.

He beckoned her in.

'So you'll fax it?' Willenheim yelled.

'Yes, sir.'

'I'm waiting.'

'Today, sir. No problem.'

'And I've got nothing to worry about?' Willenheim asked.

'Absolutely nothing.'

'Well, thank Christ for that – for your sake as much as mine. Ang Lee's on board and he's talking it through with de Niro.'

Mitch dropped into a chair and frowned. This had gone far enough. Who exactly was he trying to kid? He didn't have a hope of salvaging this situation. It would be better if he came clean. His career at Pacific was clearly over, but if he came clean now and Pacific secured the film else-where, he might still be able to work in Hollywood.

'Sir. Mr Willenheim, erm—'

He looked up at Milly, who was smiling at him. She had a beautiful warm smile, which appeared to be urging him to be strong.

'What is it, Carmichael? Don't waste my time.'

'I think de Niro would be great, sir.'

What was he thinking? It was as if *he* was playing a part in a goddamn movie.

'Carmichael, tell this writer she's creating a fucking storm over here.'

'I will, sir. I'm having dinner with her tonight.'

Mitch hung up and looked at Milly. 'I don't suppose you'd like to have dinner with me tonight, would you?' he asked.

He was poleaxed. He couldn't believe what he'd just asked her. He had twelve hours to save his life and he had asked a stranger out to dinner.

'I'd love to,' she said, looking as dumbfounded as him.

CHAPTER TWELVE

Muriel was sitting cross-legged in an easy chair, laughing hysterically. She had decided to read Juliet's script the moment she'd put the phone down on her earlier today. She felt bad about the way Lyal was treating her, and understood why she'd been upset. She'd been remarkably patient not to have snapped before now. And Muriel was delighted that she'd quickly read it because she'd loved it. What an imagination! As soon as Lyal got back from his protracted lunch, she was going to tell him what a brilliant script he had on his hands and what a wonderful film it would make. He shouldn't be long now, after all, the day was all but over.

Right on cue, he skulked in. 'Oh, Lyal, you're back,' she said.

'Yes,' he snarled.

'Have you read Juliet's script yet?'

'Juliet?'

'Phillips.'

'Oh, God, she hasn't phoned again, has she?'

'No.'

'And you've cancelled the meeting?'

'Yes. Have you read it?' Muriel repeated.

'No, of course not. Why do you think I cancelled the meeting?'

'Well, you should. It's stunning.'

'How do you know?' he asked, irritated.

'Because I've just read it. Lyal, it's great. You'd love it.'

'Look, Muriel, I'm the agent here, I'll decide what's brilliant. I'll read it in my own good time, okay. And please don't start letting my clients bully you because that's the last thing I need. Do you understand?'

'Yes, Lyal.' You smug little shit.

'George, it's me.'

'Actually, Milly, I'm a bit tied up at the moment. Can I ring you back?'

Georgina was in the middle of writing an important pitch for a new client that had to be delivered first thing tomorrow morning.

'You'll never guess what's happened,' Milly said.

'Milly, I'm really—'

'Guess who I'm having dinner with tonight?'

'Oh, I don't know – George Clooney, Steven Spielberg.'

'Come on, don't be silly.'

'Who, then? I've got a deadline!'

'Mitch Carmichael.'

'Who?' Georgina asked.

'You know, the film executive. The one from this morning.'

'Oh, my God. The cute one?'

'Yes!'

'Wow. How? Why? I mean, this morning you hate him, now you're having dinner – it's like you're married already. How did *that* happen?' It seemed that Georgina's deadline had just been extended.

'It was weird. I was in his room, right—' Milly began.

'You were in his *room*? You're a receptionist. What were you doing in *there*?'

'I'm trying to explain.' Milly giggled. 'I was expecting him to sign for a fax, but he was on the phone and he invited me in.'

'And you went? Just like that?'

'Yeah.'

'God, you tart! I had no idea you were so desperate,' Georgina said. 'Don't tell me, he was just wearing his Calvin's.'

'Don't be stupid.'

'Not *Y-fronts*?'

'Oh, George, shut up! Anyway, he looked totally worn out and whoever he was on the phone to was giving him a serious bollocking. He'd got the phone away from his ear.'

'So what did you do?' Georgina asked.

'I just smiled at him.'

'Good move. You've always had a lovely smile, you lucky bitch. Then what?'

'He said *I'm having dinner with her tonight*, put the phone down, looked up at me and asked *me* to dinner.'

'Way ta go, Milly. Your bloody boat's come in at long last. This could solve both the problems that are your life.'

'I don't think so,' Milly said, with almost everything crossed.

'Where are you meeting?'

'I was so flustered I suggested here at the hotel.'

'What about Mahmood?'

'He'll hit the roof.'

'Tell him it's all part of the new five-star deluxe service.'

Milly laughed. 'Yeah, service with a moan. I suppose I owe you a thank-you.'

'Oh, don't be silly. Although you will after our trip out. I can meet you in, say, fifteen, twenty minutes?'

'What? Meet where? Why?' Milly asked.

'God, Milly, do I have to spell it out for you?'

'Well, yes.'

'Big date – you'll need an outfit, right?'

'Er—'

'Harvey Nichols, fifteen minutes. And yes, I'll make a call, see if I can get you in at the salon.'

'I'm not getting married, George. We're just going for dinner.'

'So you're going to show up in your hotel uniform, are you? Milly, this is a new-outfit night if ever there was one, and I'm giving you my fashion guidance and time free of charge.'

'What about your deadline?'

'What deadline? Harvey Nicks, twenty minutes.'

Milly and Georgina pushed their way through the heavy double doors of Harvey Nichols and were relieved to feel the blast of cool air. They ran the gauntlet of the cosmetics department, dodging heavily made-up women armed with an array of wonder products that promised the world and delivered nothing.

'The vamp section's through here,' Georgina said, and steered a path to the couture department.

A beautiful leggy woman galloped over. 'Georgina,

lovely to see you, darling. And so soon.' The two women almost kissed each other four times then laughed at nothing in particular. She was called Anastasia, and kept her eyes shut for most of the greeting, probably so Milly couldn't see the pound signs flashing within them.

'Anastasia, this is my beautiful friend Milly. Tonight Milly's got the date of her life, so she needs to look incredibly sexy,' Georgina gushed.

'Oh, how exciting! Anyone I know?'

'George . . .' Milly pleaded.

'Please, Milly, couture, this is my department,' Georgina said, with no irony, as Anastasia looked on. Not that Anastasia minded, of course. Georgina could have said anything at all, apart from 'Thanks, I think I'll leave it', and it would have been okay with Anastasia.

'Well, Milly,' said Anastasia, 'you look gorgeous anyway, but I'm sure I've got something that will make you look divine.'

'Thank you,' Milly said. What is the divine look these days? she wondered. Wings and a halo?

Anastasia looked her up and down then assumed a pose to indicate that she was deep in thought. Somewhere in her head a light went on. 'I've got it! I have the most amazing Stella McCartney outfit that's *just* come in.'

'Oh, that sounds great, Tasie. Milly, darling, you like Stella McCartney, don't you?' Georgina asked.

'Dunno! Never met her,' Milly answered facetiously, as 'Tasie' cantered off to fetch the outfit. She was back in a flash with a sliver of silk fabric over her arm. The Stella McCartney number was a gold chiffon dress.

'Oh, Tasie! This is absolutely fabulous!' Georgina said,

and held it up to herself. Did she actually say 'absolutely fabulous'? Or was Milly having a weird dream?

'Isn't it divine?' Anastasia agreed. 'It's Italian raw silk.'

Milly groaned inwardly. Oh well, if it's Italian silk, then give it here. She often wondered how it was that everything Italian was considered superior. Coffee, shoes, clothes, footballers, ham, bread and now even their silk worms had made it into the special list. Milly sighed. There was no way her budget would stretch to Ms McCartney's efforts. Hotel receptionists didn't usually feature in the *Sunday Times* rich list.

'Milly, don't say a word, until you've tried it on,' Georgina urged.

In the fitting room, Milly noted that the price tag was conspicuously absent, but she didn't panic because she wasn't going to buy it. For all her reservations, though, the dress fitted and felt wonderful, and Milly grudgingly admitted that it looked pretty good too. She turned around and admired her slim exposed back, still brown from her holiday in Sicily. However, no matter how good she looked, nothing could have prepared her for the impact it would have on Georgina and Aniseed, or what-ever her stupid name was.

'Oh, Milly!' Georgina gushed. Anaesthesia held her breath and both her breasts and Georgina looked as if she were about to cry.

'For God's sake, George, it's only a dress.'

'Have you ever modelled?' Anodyne asked – doubtless it was a line she used at least once a day.

'Just as a matter of interest, how much is it?' Milly asked.

Anagram gasped at the enquiry before going off to

check. In the couture section of Harvey Nichols one can just assume that everything is reassuringly expensive.

Aneurysm returned looking as if she were about to tell a homeowner that she'd just run over their cat.

'Two thousand eight,' she said. 'But as you're with Georgina I could let you have ten per cent off.'

Milly burst out laughing, turned on her heel and went back to remove the dress, which was worth twice as much as her car.

When she came back, Amnesia had gone. Fortunately, she had spotted another customer suffering from a chronic shortage of self-esteem.

Georgina said, 'Milly, whatever you want to wear, price isn't an issue because I'm paying.'

'No way!'

'I brought you here, so I'm paying. Not another word. In any case, we're both celebrating.'

'Are we?' Milly asked.

'Yes. You've met your prospective husband—'

'Yeah. Right.'

'—and I'm pregnant!'

It took a split second for this momentous news to register, but then Milly screamed with delight and leapt into Georgina's arms. Her friend had been about to start IVF treatment. 'Oh, George, that's the *best* news I've had for ages.'

Androgynous bounded over to them. 'What have you found?' she gushed.

'Yes, I know it's ex-directory. I told you that!'

The phone went dead. Mitch was an angry man. He

took a series of deep breaths, then tried again.

'Hello, directories. What name, please?'

'I'm looking for the ex-directory number of a lady called Juliet Millhouse—'

'I can't give—'

'I know that.' Mitch pinched the bridge of his nose. 'Could I just explain my situation?' He'd explained it already to several other Enquiries assistants, but maybe, just maybe, this one would come through for him.

'You can, but it won't make any difference,' she said.

'Whatever I say, you won't give me the number?'

'I *can't* give it to you.'

'Why not?'

'Because I don't have it.'

'You're saying you don't actually have the number?'

'Correct.'

'Oh, that's bullshit . . .'

Dead line.

What a day! To have come so close yet still be as far away as ever. It was half past seven, half an hour before he was due to leave to have dinner with a woman he didn't even know, and the last thing he needed was to have to make small talk with a wannabe writer. But he didn't have anything better to do. For all he knew, Claudia was having lunch with Juliet Millhouse right now, being careful not to spill their champagne on the recently signed contract.

'Would a Mr Clarke make himself known to a member of the cabin crew, please?' The announcement came over the Tannoy on the Virgin flight somewhere over Greenland.

Jonson thought he'd heard it correctly but he wasn't sure. There might be another Clarke on board and, no doubt, a more important one than himself.

Bing bong.

Jonson's ears pricked up again.

'Would Mr Jonson Clarke please make himself known to a member of the cabin crew?'

Bloody hell. Bit late for an upgrade now, wasn't it? A particularly effeminate purser was to hand but Jonson didn't like to flag him down. He was a big hit with the gay community and he didn't want to raise the poor bloke's hopes. He caught the eye of a stewardess whose label said she was Marie. 'I'm Jonson Clarke,' he announced, as if he were Spartacus. His fertile imagination was running wild and increasingly spectacular scenarios raced through his mind.

Maybe the captain was dead.

I've got a simulator on my PC . . . these things can't be that different.

Perhaps it was a medical emergency.

Stand aside. Grade C O-level biology coming through. I am going to have to deliver the baby myself. It's twins. Hey, no problem.

Or it could be that the landing gear had not come down.

Stand back. I'm going to crawl along the wing and push the wheel down myself.

Whatever it was, he wasn't about to let anyone down. Some four hundred people were depending on him.

'Mr Clarke,' Marie said quietly, not wanting to wake the passenger next to him, 'there's a telephone call for you. Would you mind coming to the front of the plane?'

A telephone call! On a plane! How cool was *that*? Jonson knew how to play this: like it was no big deal. That would impress everyone, including the lovely Marie. He joined her in the aisle and smiled at her. 'Is there anywhere my office can't find me, huh?' he said, and hurried up the aisle.

He was handed the receiver by the purser. Marie joined him. 'Hello. This is Jonson Clarke.'

'Are you courier 8192?'

'Er . . . yes, I believe so.'

'Your job has been cancelled. You are not *under any circumstances* to deliver that package. Can you confirm, please, that you understand this?'

'Yes. That's okay. I agree to that. You have my authorisation. Yes.'

''Scuse me?'

'Is that all?' Jonson asked brusquely, like a true CEO of a major corporation, although he was wearing jeans, a T-shirt and sitting in economy.

'So you'll not be delivering the package?'

'That's correct.'

'Your hotel bookings are the same. We'll notify you of the first available return flight.'

Jonson put down the phone, and looked at Marie. 'Who said mergers were easy?'

The ex-directory J. Millhouse to whom Mitch was so desperate to speak was a fairly well-known British television presenter. Since various high-profile stalking cases, and in response to public calls for action, the

Metropolitan Police had launched Operation Stag, an initiative to combat harrassment, focusing particularly on nuisance telephone calls. All managers from the various directory-enquiry networks had been asked to report callers who tried to secure the ex-directory number of a notable person. Detective Inspector Mark Wilkinson was in charge of the telephone division of Stag, which he resented bitterly. It was slow and unglamorous work: in the three months the operation had been running, he had had little to investigate and he and his men were desperate for some action. Mitch's arrival on the scene was manna from heaven. Usually Wilkinson spent his time dealing with over-enthusiastic call-centre supervisors, of whom David Barley was one. He worked on the Isle of Wight and loved being involved in Operation Stag. He reported everything he considered even mildly suspicious. He even called Scotland Yard to report that he had nothing to report. But it seemed that now Barley had something for DI Wilkinson: he'd reported that an American man had been enquiring after an ex-directory number for a certain J. Millhouse. Nothing suspicious about that, until the man had become aggressive and eventually said something like, 'Listen, buddy, she doesn't know me, but I know she really wants to. Hell, I've flown six thousand miles to see her.'

As a precaution, Wilkinson flagged up the name J. Millhouse to the supervisors of the ten call centres dotted around Britain and got back some unexpected results. Indeed, an American man had made five calls requesting the number of a Ms Millhouse. The contacts all confirmed that he started off polite but quickly became aggressive and abusive. Wilkinson didn't want to get over-hopeful, but it appeared that Operation Stag was about to clash horns. An emergency memo was sent to all directory-enquiry services, instructing that a supervisor be called immediately should anyone make an enquiry about J. Millhouse. Now they just had to hope that this loser tried again.

Milly settled on a simple chiffon dress by Nicole Fahri, which cost a staggering four hundred pounds. True to her word, Georgina paid, and Milly was both overwhelmed and embarrassed. 'Thanks again, George.'

'Stop thanking me, will you? You look gorgeous in it. He won't be able to resist you. And whatever happens you call me and let me know how it goes. Doesn't matter how late it is. Just call.'

'Give David a hug for me and tell him I'm thrilled about the baby. I hope it's twins.'

They hugged each other and Milly turned to walk through the park back to Park Lane. She hadn't been on a date with a fanciable man for ages, and this one was a film executive to boot. She was bloody terrified.

The euphoria she had felt at hearing Georgina's news and getting dressed in her new outfit vanished as she entered the hotel and remembered that she'd agreed to meet him in Reception. There couldn't be a worse place for her to meet a man: fraternising with guests was strictly against hotel policy, and it was inconceivable that Mr Mahmood wouldn't find out. Lucas was covering for her and he'd only agreed to do so once she had explained her predicament. She'd made him promise he wouldn't tell a soul, and it had cost her dear: a whole weekend off next month, and he'd still made her feel like he was doing her a favour.

She went to the Park Bar, and gulped down about ten pounds' worth of water.

'Would you like another drink, Miss Milly?'

'No, thank you, Halim.'

'Something stronger?'

'No, thank you.'

'Good luck with the film man.'

Bloody Lucas! He might have held off at least until after it had happened.

Ten past eight. Perhaps he'd forgotten. He was in the film business, after all. I must be bloody mad! What do I call him – Mitch? Mr Carmichael? Sir? Do I shake his hand? Do I kiss him? Her hands were clammy with perspiration. How attractive.

Suddenly Mitch was at Reception. He was fairly casually dressed, in the official uniform of the American man at play. A pair of loose trousers, expensive-looking loafers and a long-sleeved polo shirt. He looked harassed and unrelaxed, but adorable too, which made her even more nervous. She dragged her palms over the velour cushions on the sofa and made her way over to him.

'God, it's you again,' she said, when she was just behind him. It was a joke, a reference to when they'd met earlier, but Mitch looked puzzled. He hadn't got it. It wasn't the start she'd been hoping for. 'Sorry. I keep doing this, don't I?' she floundered. 'Hello, again . . . I'm Milly.' She held out her damp paw.

He smiled at her and took it. 'I'm Mitch. That, er, "God, it's you" thing.'

'Sorry about that.'

'I get it now.'

'You do?'

'Yeah. Back-reffing to earlier, right?'

'Got it in two. It would've been funny if you'd got it straight away, honest.'

'Sure. Look, I'm sorry, but I'm whacked right now . . .'

Milly's heart sank. He was going to cry off.

'. . . what with the flight, the delay and some other stuff, so I'm not too quick on the uptake. You might have to nod when you make a joke.'

Milly nodded. She was so relieved she could have hugged him. 'That wasn't a joke. That nod, I mean. That was just me agreeing.'

Mitch laughed. 'I'm slow, but not that slow,' he said.

'Well, then, we're going to get on great,' she said, smiling again. Remarkably, her nerves had all but disappeared. She felt at ease, confident even. Then she remembered how important it was to get herself and Mitch out of the hotel. 'Where shall we go?' she asked.

'We can eat here.' He gestured to the restaurant.

'*No!*' she squeaked.

'Why? Is it that bad?' he joked.

A sense of humour too. Bloody hell. Was he perfect or what? 'No, it's not that. But we should go out – you know, what with me working here . . .' Milly tailed off. 'Not that we're . . . you know . . .'

'Okay, I know exactly what you're saying.' Mitch guffawed. 'Like I said, I'm a little slow on the uptake right now. So, Milly, it's your town. Where do you suggest?'

Such an obvious question and Milly had overlooked it. Why didn't I ask George? She would have known.

Mitch seemed to sense her discomfort. 'Hey, I tell you what, when I'm in London, we always eat at this one place. Scott's. Do you know it?'

Milly wondered whether she could get away with lying. 'Scott's.' She pretended to think about it.

'It's in Mayfair.'

Oh, like that's going to help. I'm always eating in Mayfair. 'Er, I think I *might* have been there . . .'

'You'll remember it when you see it again.'

Scott's was a suitably exclusive-looking restaurant on Mount Street, in Mayfair, a little down from the Grosvenor House Hotel. Mitch was recognised at the door by the restaurant equivalent of Anastasia, and they were led to a cosy table by the window. Milly felt giddy as Claus, their waiter, eased a comfortable chair into the back of her legs. She looked out on to the street, which was strewn with expensive cars. This had the makings of a perfect evening. What she wouldn't give now to have Elliot, her ex-husband, walk past and clock her.

'Milly, the fish here is fantastic. Is white wine okay?'

Milly nodded. Anything you want, Mr Gorgeous Chops.

'We'll have a bottle of the Petit Chablis. Fizzy or still?'

Milly stared at him, confused.

'The water.'

'Oh, I'm sorry, I thought you meant the wine. Erm,

still, please. And what were you saying about being slow?'

Mitch laughed.

'I've had a tough day too,' she added.

'Well, I can categorically assure you that it hasn't been as calamitous as mine.'

'Okay, then, I challenge you to who had the hardest day,' Milly said.

'It'll be a no-contest.'

It was a competition she couldn't possibly win. She was having a great day. The best day she'd had since *Artistic Licence* was first borrowed. Her best friend was pregnant, great news in anyone's book, and she was having dinner with an outrageously attractive man. Not that she could admit that to him, of course.

'Are you over here on business or pleasure?' she asked.

'At the moment, I'd have to say pleasure. But actually I'm here on business. That business being trying to save my career.'

Claus arrived with the drinks and filled their glasses. 'Would you care to order now, sir?'

Although neither of them had looked at the menu, Mitch seemed keen to get on with it. 'Milly, just pick whatever. Everything's fabulous here.'

She scanned the sumptuous list of fish extravaganzas, and settled on the Dover sole. It was her dad's favourite meal, and so she always set out to like it as well.

'So that's two mussels to start, then monkfish and a Dover sole. Very good, sir.' Claus disappeared.

'So you're looking to save your film career, and I'm looking to start mine,' Milly said.

'Well, I expect the odds are with you,' Mitch responded.

'Now you're going to have to explain that,' she said.

'Well, you're a début writer, right?'

'Right.'

'First screenplay?'

'Second.'

'How far did the first get?'

'Optioned, and bought by a studio,' Milly said proudly, 'but then it died.'

'That's great. You did real well. Most don't even get read.'

'And the dying part?'

'That's normal as well, I'm afraid, but you're a good few rungs up the ladder. You know you can write. You got an agent?'

'Sort of.'

'He's crap, right?' Mitch laughed.

'Completely.'

'They all are. Doesn't return your calls?'

She nodded.

'He will. When you make it he'll be a great agent.'

'*If* I make it.'

'You will. I'm sure of it. Perhaps not with your first or second. Probably not even your third—'

'How many do I have to write?'

'As many as it takes. M. Knight Shylaman—'

'*The Sixth Sense*. I loved that film,' Milly said.

'Of course, one of the best in the last ten years. But that was his eighth script.'

'Oh, great! And this is you trying to encourage me? There's no way I've got the energy for another six. Why do I bother?'

''Cos if you guys didn't, I wouldn't have a job.'

'So I'll do it for you then. Just to save your career.'

'I think I'm a little late for that. I need a miracle.'

'So you'd better tell me. Remember our contest.'

'Okay. I'm head of Development at Pacific Studios, and there's this script in the States at the moment that's just so hot. Everyone wants it, including my boss, and for some reason he thinks I've developed it.'

'And you haven't?'

'No. I've never even seen it. But I've told him I have. But I don't even know who wrote it. And if Willenheim finds that out, I'm history.'

'Willenheim?' Milly said.

'Yeah. Albert T. Willenheim. Major player in LA.'

'He stayed at the hotel with you, didn't he?'

'That's right, yeah. Big guy – real good-looking.'

Milly was bewildered until Mitch burst out laughing.

'He's a very powerful man. If I screw this up, I'm on TV game shows for the rest of my life. Please tell me when I start to bore you.'

That was highly unlikely, she thought. 'I remember him now. Quite a scary guy.'

''Scuse me. He is Hollywood's *most* scary man, and guess who's really pissed him off.'

Milly's mind drifted off with the romance of his story. She tried to imagine how wonderful it must be to have written a script that half of Hollywood wanted. 'It must be fantastic to have written a script like that,' she mused aloud.

'And even more fantastic if I could sign it.'

'Have you tried the agents?'

Mitch chuckled. 'Milly, thank God I've met you . . . Here, eat my fish, I've got phone calls to make.'

'All right, all right. And I thought the Americans had no sense of irony.'

'No. The irony is that you guys think we don't get it.'

'I like that.'

'Favourite sit-com?'

She thought about it. Her instincts were urging her to go with something obvious, something safe, a *Frasier* or a *Simpsons*, but she decided to go for honesty.

'*Spin City*.'

'Hey, me too.'

It was now official. This guy was perfect.

'Okay. So you're looking for the writer. How come you're in London?'

'Ah, man, I feel like such a chump now. I thought I'd found my writer.' Mitch filled her in on his disastrous movie purchase from Joo-Leigh.

Milly was aghast.

'And it was Willenheim I was talking to, or listening to, when you showed up.'

'You didn't tell him!'

'No, 'course not. Do I look mad? Told him I was having dinner with the writer tonight and here I am.'

'I'm flattered.' She smiled. 'Well, then, maybe you should read my script.'

'Send it to me in LA and I promise I'll read it when I get back. And if I've still got a job I'll put some heat your way with your agent.'

'I doubt even you could do that.'

'Who is he?'

'Lyal Roberts.'

Mitch laughed as an army of waiters cleared away their plates. He waited for the last one to sweep the tablecloth clean before continuing.

'I know Lyal. Little bit grandiose, but he's a good agent.'

'So people keep telling me.'

'Looks after Dylan Walsh.'

'Yeah, okay. Don't keep going on,' Milly joked.

'What you have to understand is that agents spend most of their time trying to keep their—'

'Successful clients happy,' Milly interrupted, smiling so that he would know she wasn't offended.

'Anyway, how come you had a bad day?' Mitch asked.

Lyal cancelling her meeting seemed utterly trivial now, and Milly decided she couldn't compete. 'Oh, compared to yours it was a dream. So, what's this writer's name, then?'

With appalling timing, Claus appeared, wheeling over the most magnificent sweet trolley Milly had ever seen. He whipped through the desserts that were on offer and the question she'd asked moments ago was forgotten amidst the calorific extravaganzas.

'Chocolate roulade, please,' Milly said.

The waiter loaded a bowl with an embarrassingly large portion.

'Cream, madaarm?'

'If there's any room,' she joked.

'Anything else for you, madaarm?' he asked.

'Yes, a Stair Master.'

Claus didn't get the joke but Mitch laughed heartily.

'And for you, sir?'

'Just the fruit salad, please. No cream, thank you.'

It would have been embarrassing for her if he hadn't started laughing again as she caught his eye.

'No, I was just joking. I'd love some of the roulade as well . . . if there's any left, of course.'

It was after eleven when they left the restaurant, and neither of them wanted the evening to end.

'Do you know I've been coming to London for nearly ten years now,' Mitch said, 'and I've never seen it. I've been in most of the movie offices in Soho, but I've never really been round the City.'

'Well, the City is just banks and offices. Except for St Paul's Cathedral, of course.'

'I'd love to see it. Could we walk there?'

'It'd take all night.'

'Then let's get a cab. Could we do that? London taxi-drivers. Friendliest cabbies in the world, right?'

Milly frowned.

'You can show me St Paul's and all the other sights. What do you say?'

'I'd love to.'

He offered Milly his arm, which she took, and they set off to search for a cab. Mayfair is never short of cabs and they were soon travelling through the West End. Mitch was like a little boy visiting Disneyland. Practically every building to him was an historical wonder. Even Piccadilly Circus captivated him, which surprised her given that he came from the country that had given the world Las Vegas.

'Wow. That's beautiful. What's that?'

Milly looked up at another white-and-grey stone affair. All lit up, it was a very impressive building, but she didn't have a clue what it was.

'Erm, it's probably a bank or something like that.'

It was immediately apparent that Milly was only going to be able to point out the postcard sites. Pretending to be disgusted with her, Mitch leaned forward and tapped the glass. ''Scuse me, driver . . . Do you do tours?'

'What, gov?'

'Would you just drive around, pointing out sites to us?'

'I'm a bloody taxi-driver, mate, not a tour guide,' the cabbie said angrily.

'I'll give you a hundred pounds more than your meter says at the end of the ride.'

The cab speeded up.

'On your left is the famous Lloyds building, designed by . . .'

The tour had begun in earnest.

At just after 1 a.m., the taxi pulled up outside the Shelton Tower.

'This is the Shelton Tower, Park Lane. Built in the 1850s . . .' Milly began. Mitch laughed.

'Milly. It's been a fantastic night, and London's such a beautiful city.'

Suddenly they were silent. He had to pay off the

gargantuan cab bill, but an awkward moment loomed. Milly's heart was racing. She didn't know what to hope for or what to expect. A kiss goodnight at the very least, but what kind of kiss? Her nervousness was back with a vengeance.

Mitch got out and paid off the cab-driver, then said, 'I need you to take my friend home to . . .' He glanced at Milly.

'South Ealing,' she said.

'How much to Ealing?' Mitch asked.

'Maybe firty-five quid.'

'There's another forty. I don't want you dropping her off short now, you hear?'

'Much obliged, chief.'

Mitch came back to the passenger door. He held out his hands. She took them and they kissed.

Milly's heart almost leapt out of the cab after him: the kiss had a definite 'to be continued' feel about it. Which was as infuriating now as it had been when she was a kid and it flashed up on the screen at the end of *Charlie's Angels*. This time, she was determined not to miss the concluding episode.

'Milly, it's been a wonderful evening. For a while I forgot I had any problems.'

'So we should do it again, unless you solve your problems, of course.'

'Even if I solve my problems. You at work tomorrow?'

For the first time ever, Milly was looking forward to it. 'Yep.'

'Good. I'll see you then.'

The taxi pulled away from the hotel. She wanted to

turn round to see whether he was waving, but she didn't: she didn't want to appear too keen. She laughed to herself. Bolts, stable doors and horses sprang to mind, but she didn't care: she hoped it was obvious how she felt – it would save her the embarrassment of telling him. Now she needed some sleep, but she had an idea that she wouldn't get much.

CHAPTER THIRTEEN

Feeling tired and grubby, Jonson headed through the nothing-to-declare channel at Los Angeles International. The airport was like all others he'd ever visited throughout the world, except that it was the airport of the stars, and Jonson wondered whose footsteps he was treading in as he made his way across the highly polished floor. Sinatra, Stallone, Schwarzenegger, Jackson, Cruise, Eastwood, Redford. People so famous they only needed one name. A list of luminaries now supplemented by Clarke, Jonson Clarke. It made him feel even more important than he normally did approaching the sliding arrivals door in an airport. Forget Warhol's fifteen minutes of fame – the entry into the arrivals hall of an airport affords everyone a fleeting glimpse of true star status.

Eddie Murphy had been on Jonson's flight, cocooned in the first-class cabin with his entourage, and whispers spread among the airport paparazzi that a meal ticket had just landed. Lenses and ladders gathered at the arrivals hall, which itself attracted a swell of curious onlookers. As the doors opened, Jonson, the black man in a baseball cap, was instantly mistaken for the movie star and was duly greeted by a barrage of flashbulbs. Though he couldn't understand the sudden interest in him, he loved the attention and was happy to look this way and that. However, within seconds they realised their mistake and the commotion died away. From movie star to nobody in an instant. Jonson now had an inkling of how it felt to be Jean-Claude Van Damme.

Bewildered, he spotted a woman holding a notice with his name on it. He went over to her. She asked for identification, then handed him an envelope. Jonson opened it. A hotel booking for the Holiday Inn on West and 34th, with a return flight for 10 a.m. Tuesday. He smiled. Two whole days in LA.

In the small hours of the morning the hotel was relatively quiet, and Mitch made for the reception desk. He didn't get that far.

'Misster Carmichael.'

Mitch turned to see an odd little man approaching him at great speed. He came to an abrupt ramrod halt and a little hand shot out at Mitch as if activated by a lever.

'We haven't met. I'm Misster Mahmood, manager of the Shelton Tower, Park Lane.' He bowed slightly. 'Welcome back to the hotele – not tonight, I mean back here since your last visit. I trust everything is to your liking.'

'Absolutely.'

'You had a nice evening? I trust Mill-ee is looking after you.'

Mitch looked at the man suspiciously. He didn't want to compromise Milly, but he reasoned that a lie might do that just as easily as the truth. 'Yes. We had a lovely evening, thank you.'

Mr Mahmood's eyes widened and Mitch's worst fears were confirmed. Milly had broken the rules and she was in trouble. 'There's no problem with us having a meal out, is there?' he asked.

Mr Mahmood was shaking his head vigorously, but Mitch was not convinced.

'Because if there is, I can always check into the Lanesborough,' he said. He hadn't thought it possible that the little man's eyes could open even wider, and he steadied himself to catch his eyeballs should they roll out of his head.

'No! Absolutely not! I wouldn't hear of it,' Mr Mahmood said. 'No. No. I just wantedd to make sure that we are all doing all we can to make your stay a pleasant one.'

'Thank you, I appreciate that.'

'You have a lott of messages.' Mr Mahmood gestured to the night receptionist, who held up a sheaf of paper.

Mitch's spirits took a deep, spiralling dive.

Milly wondered whether Georgina had really meant she should call at any time. It was almost 2.00. But, knowing Georgina, she had. Milly dialled her friend's number. The phone was answered immediately.

'And?' Georgina answered. She must have been waiting for the call.

'I have just had the *most* fantastic night.'

'What happened?'

'We went for a meal and—'

'Somewhere nice?'

'Scott's. Do you know it?'

'Yes, of course I do. What about afterwards?'

'George!'

'Oh, *come on*!'

'He kissed me goodnight.'

'Is that it?'

'Yes.'

'Oh, blimey! And you thought you should call!'

'You told me—'

'I know, I know. I'm only joking. Well, what sort of kiss was it?'

'A normal one.'

'Normal? What does that mean?'

'On the lips, but long enough for it to be more than just friendly.'

'So what's he like?'

'Totally gorgeous. Nice bloke, funny, kind, good fun . . .'

'All right, all right. That's enough! Remember who's lying next to me – I might get jealous.' Milly heard a reproachful male grunt.

'Look, it's late,' she said. 'I'll let you go. Thanks again for everything.'

'Call you tomorrow.'

Milly put the phone down. Once again sleep seemed like a remote possibility.

As he looked at his messages in the lift, it was clear to Mitch that some well-deserved shut-eye wasn't an option. Two from Scott, one from Josie, one from his ex-wife, one from Dolores, and one from Jerry Greene, an ambitious and odious lawyer from Legal. No sooner had

Mitch closed his door behind him than his phone rang.

'Hello.'

'Oh, my God, so you're still alive, then?' Jerry Greene said.

Mitch regretted picking up the phone. 'Jerry. Hi. How nice to hear from you – at two in the morning.'

'Well, Mitch, you chose to go to London without telling anyone.'

The two men had never liked each other, which was a shame for Mitch because Jerry had reserved a seat for himself at the boardroom table and it was always good to have friends at that level. Not that it seemed relevant to Mitch now. By the time Jerry made the board, Mitch doubted that he would still be in the business.

'How can I help you, Jerry?'

'Where to start? There's so much you could do for so many people here right now. By the way, thanks for the contract you faxed through. The *Untitled* one.'

Mitch braced himself.

'Made us look like a right bunch of assholes, didn't you? Why did you fax it straight to Willenheim?'

'Just following orders,' Mitch said, his conscience surprisingly clear.

'Well, you should have faxed us a copy too. Willenheim tore a strip off Dylan. I'm tellin' you, man, he's fuckin' freakin' out.'

Mitch rolled his eyes. Dylan Tizer, head of Legal, was not an enemy anyone would choose to make but, given what Mitch was already up against, it made little difference to him.

'Do you know what's going down here, Mitch?'

'No, but I figure you're calling to tell me,' Mitch said defiantly.

'This contract isn't worth shit, and the word is that you haven't got any script or any writer. I've got fuckin' journalists from *Variety* phoning me up asking all kinds of questions. They wanna run a story to find this fuckin' writer. What have you got to say about that, huh?'

Mitch gulped. 'They've got no story,' he said.

'This writer. I hear you had dinner with her tonight.'

'That's right.'

'Oh. And how did it go?' Jerry didn't wait for a reply. He was famed for his aggression: he had modelled himself on any number of attorneys he'd seen in movies. His questions were designed to make a point rather than solicit information, which suited Mitch because he didn't have any information to give. 'Dylan Tizer doesn't like having to threaten *Variety* with legal action. It's not great for promoting our studio and movies.'

'No, I can see that.'

'I take it you know Claudia's joined Columbia and word is that they're about to make some sort of announcement. If they have that movie, my advice is stay in London, pal.'

The remnants of Mitch's confidence evaporated. This was an outright disaster. His mouth was as dry as the towels in his bathroom and he thanked God for the minibar. Frantically he opened a bottle of Highland Spring. He would have drained it if it hadn't been fizzy.

'Jerry, I know how this might seem but—'

'Oh, well, that's great. As long as you know how it seems, I guess we can all relax. I'll tell everyone to stop panicking, shall I?' Evidently Jerry was enjoying this. 'So how is our writer?' he asked.

'She's great.'

'Good. And *is* there any chance we might ever get to meet her? Like maybe she might come to Los Angeles? Believe me, she'd make a lot of people very happy and, as you know, we'd treat her like a princess. I mean, what's up with the girl? Most writers kill to get here. What is she? Some sort of wacko?'

Mitch wondered whether keeping up this pretence was worth while. Should he just come clean? It'd certainly be fun: *'Hey, listen up, Jerry, you smug shit. I haven't got a clue who this writer is. Did you get that, Jerry? You little fuckin' worm. That contract I faxed through, I signed it. It ain't worth shit. So yeah! You should be worried. For all I know, Columbia have already signed her. And do you know something else? I hope they have. And, Jerry, you might as well drop your pants and spread your legs because you can shove my job up your ass.'*

But Mitch didn't have the courage for such bravado, which, after all, was the stuff of movies.

'So! When can I tell my bosses to expect you?' Jerry asked.

'I expect to be back in LA within the next couple of days or—'

'No offence intended, Mitch, but it's not you we wanna see. I take it Juliet will be with you?'

'Of course. Believe me, I'm working on her.'

Mitch cut him off and dialled Scott.

'Scott, it's me.'

'Where have you been? I've been trying to get hold of you for hours.'

'Have you found her?' Mitch asked desperately.

'No. Have you?'

'No.'

'Did you know Cameron Diaz is on board?'

'Shit, Scott, who cares? I just got off the phone with Jerry Greene.'

'Mitch, I know you know this, but you need some answers and quick.'

'Which is why I've gotta ring off, Scott.'

He hung up and dialled another number immediately.

'Directories. What name, please?'

'Millhouse. J. Millhouse.'

'Hold the line, sir.'

Mitch waited patiently. Eventually the operator spoke again. 'Sorry about that, sir. How can I help you?'

'J. Millhouse. There's an ex-directory listing for a J. Millhouse. Now, I know you're not allowed to give me that number.'

'That's correct.'

'So what do I have to do to get it?'

'You mean . . .'

'Yes. How much do you want? Say, a thousand pounds – two thousand?'

There was silence at the other end of the line.

'Okay. Three thousand,' Mitch said frantically.

'Hello, caller . . .'

'Yes, I'm here.'

'Okay. Three thousand pounds,' the operator agreed.

'Great. I'm at the Shelton Tower, Park Lane Hotel in London. Can you get to London?'

'Yes, I live there.'

'Can we meet first thing tomorrow?'

'No, I have to take my kids to school.'

Three thousand pounds, lady. Give the kids a morning off, why don't you? 'Okay, so when's good?'

'I could get there for ten.'

'Ten's great. I'll meet you in Reception. How will I recognise you?'

'I'm in my early forties, although people think I look younger—'

'Just wear something distinctive, huh? A hat or a head-scarf.'

The woman thought for a moment. 'I'll wear a navy blue hat with a Burberry scarf.'

'Tomorrow morning, then.'

Mitch wasn't excited as he put the phone down. It was just another long-shot, and unlikely that it would be his writer anyway. The whole episode had been a cock-up from start to finish.

Milly arrived at work early, exhausted yet exhilarated at the prospect of seeing Mitch again.

Mr Mahmood intercepted her. 'Mill-ee, might I have a wordd, pliss?'

She knew what it would be about but not how best to play it. Honesty was probably the best strategy, but she couldn't see him buying the love-at-first-sight argument.

When she entered his office he was sitting behind his desk, his fingers drumming impatiently. 'Did you have a nice time last nightt?'

'Lovely, thank you,' Milly replied.

'Anything else you want to add?' he asked.

'Mr Mahmood, last night I was taken out by—'

'Mr Carmichael. We had a little chatt on his way in.' He stared at her like her dad used to when she'd got home later than the agreed time. 'Mill-ee, this is not something I approve of. Do you understand?'

'No, sir.'

'This is most irregular, taking out guests.'

'Sir, he asked me out, and I thought it would be rude to say no.'

'Mill-ee, none of the staff can know about this,' he said, but her face gave her away. 'Who already knows?' he asked crossly.

'Lucas.'

'Mr Channel Tunnel himself. Will you be seeing him againe?'

'I don't know . . . We've made no plans.'

'Well, if you mustt, no one can know about it. Do you understand?'

'Yes, sir.'

'But there is one rule I want you to observe.'

Milly nodded.

'No bonking in my hotel.'

Milly almost laughed. She had known he would be mad at her, but she hadn't expected the 'not under my roof' speech.

'Remember, Milly. This is my hotel and I'm watching you.'

'I know you are, sir. We all know you are.'

As Mitch walked across Reception to the dining room for breakfast, he and Milly stole a quick glance at each other, while Mr Mahmood looked on like a prison guard.

When he moved away, Milly seized her opportunity. She pulled an A4 envelope out of her bag and made for the dining room.

'Good morning, madam, what is your room number, please?' Fabien, the head waiter, chuckled.

'Got a package to deliver, Fabien.'

Mitch looked exhausted. He definitely hadn't had any sleep and she wondered whether it might have been for the same reasons as her. She hoped so.

'Hi, Mitch,' she said, nervously. Maybe last night hadn't been as big a deal for him as it had been for her.

She needn't have worried. He smiled at her, obviously pleased to see her, then spotted the package under her arm. 'Something for me?'

'My script. I know you said send it, but . . .'

'Save the postage, huh?'

'Absolutely. Do you know what I earn?'

'Milly, I'm not going to have time to read it until I get this thing cleared up.'

'Fine.'

'I mean it! So don't be looking at me with those big beautiful eyes of yours for some feedback.'

'Hey, no pressure – it's not my style.' She was thrilled

he thought her eyes were beautiful. Suddenly Mr Mahmood appeared in the doorway. His gaze settled on the couple in the bay window.

'Mr Mahmood, good morning,' Mitch called, waving theatrically.

Milly scuttled back to Reception. She could feel his disappointed glare upon her and could hear him repeating his golden 'no bonking' rule.

Later in the morning, Milly decided to chance another call to Lyal's office.

'Hello, Muriel. It's Juliet.'

'Juliet, I'm glad you called.'

'You are?' Milly said, sounding surprised.

'Yes. I've just read your script, and I love it.'

'You do?' Milly was thrilled. At last someone had read it.

'Yes. How did you think of it all?'

'Oh, you know . . .' Milly preferred to keep Jonson secret. 'I don't suppose Lyal's read it yet?' she asked.

'No. But I will urge him to, and I'll tell him how much I enjoyed it when I see him.' Muriel couldn't bring herself to say she'd already tried and failed.

'Thanks Muriel. That would be great.'

'He did say something about needing to talk to you, though.'

An alarm bell sounded in Milly's head. What could he want? After all these years, what could he possibly have to say? He certainly owed her an apology, but there was no way it could be that. Maybe he was in the process of culling his client list. Over the years, Lyal had proved himself spectacularly useless, but he was still marginally better than nothing. Milly decided she needed to head off this possibility.

'Would you tell Lyal I've just had a meeting with Mitch Carmichael?'

'Oh,' Muriel said, surprised. 'Mitch Carmichael at Pacific?'

'Yes. The development guy. He's asked for a copy of my script, which I've given to him, and he said he's going to call Lyal about it.'

'Juliet, that is fantastic news! I'll tell Lyal as soon as I see him.'

Milly hung up feeling invigorated. Muriel was the first professional person to have read her script and she couldn't have been more fulsome in her praise. It reaffirmed her belief that her work was good. Now perhaps Lyal might read it. That was all she'd ever asked of him.

Suddenly it occurred to her that the cover sheet on Mitch's script read 'by Juliet Millhouse', not 'by Juliet Phillips' as Lyal knew her. But it didn't matter: the title of the screenplay was the same.

The Park Bar was quiet with just a few people deliberating how best to while away the day. Mitch was sitting in the corner with a good view of the lobby, and hadn't noticed the three men sitting almost opposite him with glasses of mineral water.

At exactly ten o'clock, a middle-aged woman entered the hotel, wearing a navy beret complete with checked scarf. Mitch wasted no time. He got up to meet her in Reception, then led her into the bar. No sooner had they sat down than they were joined by the three men. Mitch looked pointedly at the empty tables and said, 'Excuse me, fellas, do you have to sit here?'

'And who are you, sir?' one asked.

'Excuse me?'

'Your name, sir?'

'Why do you want to know? What's yours?'

'Detective Inspector Wilkinson, Scotland Yard.'

'Police?'

'That's right, sir. Would you mind accompanying me to Paddington Green police station, sir?'

'There must be some mistake here.'

'It shouldn't take long, and the station would be a lot more private.'

'I'm not going anywhere until you tell me why.' Mitch caught sight of Mr Mahmood hovering just outside the door, looking like a thundercloud.

'Bribery in this country is a crime, sir.'

Mitch looked at the three officers. 'Am I being arrested?'

'Not yet, sir. No. Shall we go, sir?'

Mitch was marched through Reception with the three men forming a close triangle around him. He wasn't handcuffed, but it was apparent to everyone that he wasn't being taken on another sightseeing tour.

'I have absolutely no idea what they might have wanted,' Milly said.

'It's not drugs, is it? Tell me it's not drugs,' Mr Mahmood pleaded.

'He's a Hollywood film executive, for God's sake,' Milly said, as if that might allay his fears. 'We just had a meal, went for a drive. There must be some mistake. He seemed to be a really nice guy.'

'I will not have this hotele dragged down! First it's a prostitute, then he's trying to sleep with my staff, and now he is arrested in broad daylightt. What nextt?'

'I'm sure there's a rational explanation for everything.'

'Then, pliss, give me one.'

Milly fumbled. 'I can't, but I'm sure there *is* one.'

'New rule, Mill-ee. You let me know everything you know. As soon as you hear it.'

'Yes, sir.'

'Dismist.'

'Yes, it was me making the calls. I've already admitted to that. But I am not a star stalker. I'm a movie executive, for God's sake. I know movie stars. I meet them all the time. What would I want with a regional English television newscaster?'

This guy had classic delusional thoughts common in sad people who start stalking to fill their empty lives, Wilkinson thought. As for this nonsense about a script – Wilkinson wasn't buying that for a second. He was well and truly living with the fairies. Although DI Wilkinson did have some doubt about his new suspect: he didn't exactly fit the profile of your usual stalker – he was very good-looking and could afford a six-hundred-pound-a-night hotel suite. He was also well dressed and educated. However, the officer was trained to look beyond appearances and consider only the evidence: this guy was guilty, and his appearance only made him even more sinister. Also, he wouldn't let them make any enquiries about his story. For a start, he wouldn't tell even them which studio he worked for.

'Look, it's like I've said. Clearly this isn't the Juliet Millhouse I'm looking for. You've actually done me a favour so perhaps I should be thanking you. I'm sorry for the offence I might have caused the directories people, but can I just go and then we can all get on with our jobs?'

'And you expect me to believe this Cinderella story of yours, do you?' Wilkinson said smugly.

Mitch's patience suddenly snapped. 'Frankly, I don't give a shit what you believe. In fact, I don't give a rat's ass what anybody thinks.'

DI Wilkinson had been hoping for a smelly drifter with a twitch, living in a bed-sit full of porn with photos of his potential victim all over the walls. He didn't much like the American – the smooth, tanned skin, white teeth, foppish hair and bright blue eyes. As Carmichael was led into the station, a few WPCs had remarked that he was 'very shaggable' and had contrived reasons to visit his cell.

'You know it's against the law to try to bribe an official,' Wilkinson stated.

'Really? So arrest me, charge me, then let me go so that I can get on with my work. I really don't have time to be sitting here doing nothing with you people. I mean, shouldn't you be out catching real criminals?'

Wilkinson flinched at the insult. This was a line he'd heard over and over throughout his career, mainly from irate motorists stopped for speeding, but it always pissed him off. He stood up aggressively, pleased that his chair fell backwards with a crash.

'You think you're real smart, don't you, son?'

His suspect didn't bother to answer.

'We're not going to press any charges, so you are free to go . . .'

'Thank you, Officer,' Mitch said.

'. . . once I've processed your paperwork, which could take me – oh, it could take me all day.'

'Milly,' Lucas called. 'Phone call. I think it's that drug-dealing pimp-boyfriend of yours.'

Excited, she hurried over. 'Hello?'

'Is that Milly?'

It wasn't Mitch.

'Yes, who's that?'

'My name is Scott Tanner. I'm a colleague of Mitch's.'

'What's happened to him?'

'It's a long story. He's looking for a writer called—'

'Yes, yes, I know all this.'

'Right, okay. I'm sorry to call, but it seems that Mitch has been a little bit zealous in his search and the police think he's some kind of crazed stalker.'

Poor Mitch, she thought, and wished there was a way she could help him. 'Have they charged him?' she asked.

'No. But he's pissed off some cop and it could be this evening before he's released.'

'How can I help?'

'He asked me to call you. He's sorry but there isn't anyone else over there he knows. He needs someone to cover for him while he's with the cops.'

'Cover for him?'

'His phone calls. If the studio know why he's been busted, he's finished. I know it's a lot to ask, but Mitch said you and he had become friends—'

'Yes, we have. And, yes, I'll do it.'

'Great, he said you would.'

Did he? Confident sod.

'He also said he'd make it up to you.'

He'd better.

'The story is that you're his PA, and Mitch is tied up most of the day in a development meeting with this writer. Really, you'll just be fielding his calls.'

'Okay.'

'When people call, you'd better let me know. Especially Dolores or a guy called Willenheim – actually, just call me whoever it is.' He gave her his number.

Milly was now thinking of the practicalities. The only way she could do it would be to sit in Mitch's room all day, which would mean another day off, or at least a sickie. Either way, sitting in a guest's room all day, pretending to be his assistant and suspected of being his lover, was a sacking offence. She was being asked to risk her job to save someone else's. She'd never been a risk-taker, and she blamed the malaise of her career firmly on her safe-option shoulders. For this to work, she would need the complicity of her colleagues, which wouldn't be a problem. And frankly the prospect of doing something daring was exciting, and exactly what she needed.

Lucas was belligerent, crude, sarky, malevolent and mischievous, but he was also loyal, dependable and a good friend to Milly. He organised cover for her at Reception and swung it with Housekeeping that Mitch's suite was off limits for the day.

CHAPTER FOURTEEN

'Hello!' Mitch banged on his door. 'Hello! Is it possible that I might speak with someone, please . . .' He kicked one of the chairs gingerly, having discovered earlier, to his painful cost, that everything in the room was screwed to the floor.

Keys suddenly jangled in the lock and the door swung open. Mitch sighed as a young officer entered with a putrid cup of coffee. He was about to turn and leave without so much as a word.

'Oh, come on, man. I've been here for six hours! This is ridiculous.'

The officer turned around in the doorway to look at Mitch, but still didn't say anything. Mitch's earlier speech about how if it hadn't been for America the English would all be speaking German had obviously hit a wrong note, and it was still reverberating.

'Look, I'm sorry if I appeared rude earlier, but the release forms. Only Inspector Wilkinson can sign them, right?'

'That's right.'

'So what's the hold-up?' he shouted. 'If he's having such a hard time writing his name, couldn't you just get him a stamp? I'm sorry . . . That came out all wrong.'

'Perhaps if you weren't so rude, sir.'

'Absolutely. I'm sorry. So when do you think Inspector Wilkinson might be available to sign me out?'

'He's not here right now.'

'Well, where is he?' Mitch pleaded.

'I believe he's out catching real criminals, sir.'

The policeman smiled before triumphantly and slowly raising both his arms aloft to indicate his victory. He spun on his heel, thrilled with how he'd played the Yankee boy like a fish.

Milly enjoyed her day. She'd taken five calls and handled them all admirably. Michelle Reid called from NDR Promotions and they had a long chat about the state of film promotion in Europe. She'd call again later. No need for Mitch to call.

Jon Grisdale called from Singleton's literary agency about a client of his who had written a wonderful script called *Infidelity*. He would send it in. Milly made a separate note for herself of his details for future reference, should Lyal go through with his client cull.

Sylvia Flint called from *Entertainment Tonight* requesting an interview. Could Mitch call.

Jim Howard called from Executive Hollywood Recruitment, having heard that Mitch might be looking for a new position. His agency, he said, would love the opportunity to help him with that search. No need for Mitch to call. The vulture would call again.

And Scott wanted to know whether everything was okay. Could Mitch call him for an update?

She had also found time to tidy Mitch's suite, which had looked as if squatters had moved in when she arrived.

The phone rang again. 'Good afternoon, Mitch Carmichael's office. How can I help you?'

'Ah, hello, Lyal Roberts calling from ILM. Could I have a quick word?' he said brusquely, as if he didn't have much time and didn't want to waste it talking with an assistant.

A startled Milly scraped herself off the carpet and wondered what to do. Her mind was racing. What had she said to Muriel about Mitch reading her script?

'Hello?' she could hear coming from the mouthpiece.

'Er, yes, hello. Sorry about that . . . Sorry, sir, you are?'

'Lyal Roberts,' he growled.

'Just one moment.'

Milly had a brainwave and smiled broadly. Let's see how you like it, dickhead. 'Hello, Lyal. He's in a meeting at the moment . . .' It amused her that she'd now dropped her plummy voice and settled on her own because Lyal wouldn't have recognised it anyway. '. . . but he does need to speak to you.'

'Oh. Do you know what about?'

'He's read a script by a client of yours, which he loved . . . Now, where is it? Would you mind holding?'

'Sure.'

'Damn, I had it here a moment ago,' she said.

'*Mischievous Liaison* by Aaron Stokes?' he offered.

'No.'

'*A Passionate Crime* by Celia Holden?'

'No,' Milly said firmly.

'*The Water's Edge* by Rosalie Marshall?'

'No,' Milly said.

Lyal was quiet. The weasel was stumped: her script

wasn't on his recommended list, even though she'd told Muriel about her meeting with Mitch.

'Ah, here it is,' she said, eventually. '*Untitled* by Juliet Phillips.'

'Oh.'

'You sound surprised?'

'No . . . It's a wonderful piece. It's one of the scripts I wanted to talk to him about.'

'Has it been assigned yet?' Milly asked.

'No.'

'Have other studios and independents got it?'

'Not yet. Mitch is my first port of call.' Liar!

It was apparent he hadn't read it, but that didn't matter any more because now he *had* to read it.

'So, when can I get hold of Mitch?'

'He's got a very tight schedule,' Milly said slowly, savouring each word, 'and it might be difficult to put any more meetings in now. Why don't I have a word with him? I'll see what I can do and I'll call you back.'

Milly hung up and began to leap about the room punching the air. 'Yesss!'

'Fuck sake, busy schedule. In a meeting! What do you think I do all day, lady? Patronising bitch,' Lyal muttered. 'Muriel!' he shouted.

'Yes.'

'This blasted Juliet Phillips script. Have we got a copy?'

Muriel looked astounded. 'Of course. We've had it for months. I told you I'd read it, remember?'

'Well, get me a copy, will you?'

Muriel walked over to his desk and moved a few bundles to reveal the script.

'*Untitled*. Is that what it's called?' he asked disparagingly. It rang a distant bell in his memory but he couldn't remember why.

'It will become clear when you read it.'

'Bloody stupid name for a film.'

'You might enjoy it.'

'I doubt it. Bloody writers . . .'

At 6.25, Milly was getting out of a cab outside Paddington Green police station. The duty sergeant had explained on the phone that Mitch was due to be signed out at 6.30, and she had decided that his personal assistant should be there to greet him.

She went into the building and straight away saw Mitch walking towards her. He looked as though he'd been detained for days rather than hours. His eyes were red, his face stubbly and his hair was standing on end. His shirt was hanging out over his trousers, and his jacket was draped over his shoulder. When he spotted Milly, his face lit up. She fumbled with her skirt, not sure how to greet him. Perhaps a little hug and a peck on the cheek would be best. But Mitch held out his arms for a cuddle and she walked straight into them.

'Do all your assistants get this kind of treatment?' Milly joked, as they broke apart but still held hands.

DI Wilkinson looked on from his office. 'She's bloody fit. Lucky bastard. No wonder he wanted to get out.' He wandered out into Reception.

'Detective, it's been a pleasure meeting you and your men. No offence, of course, but I fervently hope I never see any of you again.' Then Milly and he went outside and hailed a cab.

As they meandered through the traffic towards central London, Milly gave Mitch his messages and told him about her conversation with Lyal.

'Did he realise it was you?' Mitch asked, when he'd managed to stop laughing.

'Not a clue. And I told him you'd read my script and that you loved it.'

'Way ta go! So he'll be calling me, I guess.'

'Yeah, once he's read it,' Milly answered. 'Perhaps you shouldn't take his calls for a while – make him sweat.'

But Mitch's attention had shifted. He sighed heavily. He seemed completely done in. 'What a day. But at least the wild-goose chase is over, huh?'

'What d'you mean?'

'The trail's dead. And so am I.'

'What now?' Milly asked, in trepidation.

'Who knows? Go home, come clean. See what happens.'

'Been a wasted trip for you, then.'

'Not entirely . . . I've met you. But I wish we didn't live an ocean apart.'

Milly looked at him. A lump the size of a grapefruit was wedged in her throat.

'This is gonna be my last night here so we should go out,' he said.

Milly nodded, unable to speak.

At the hotel, Samson bade them a good evening and held open the door.

'It's seven o'clock now. What d'you wanna do?' Mitch asked.

'You go and do what you need to do,' she said, 'and then get a cab to this restaurant. I'll be there at eight thirty.' She scribbled on a scrap of paper she'd pulled out of her handbag. 'Do you like Indian food?'

'Not sure if I've ever had it.'

'I think you'll love it.' She forced the paper into his breast pocket, and kissed his cheek.

By now Mr Mahmood had joined his staff in the grand-stand watching *The Milly and Mitch Show* being played out before them. Most people gasped at the kiss, but Mr Mahmood almost collapsed on to his mosaic floor. Milly turned to her boss. She was too excited and happy to be scared. Ever thoughtful, she wanted to spare him any effort. Smiling, she pointed to herself, then in the direction of his office, before setting off in that direction.

Fresh from her scolding, Milly burst out of the hotel looking forward to the night ahead. She called Georgina.

'Milly, I've been trying you for ages. Did you see him?'

'Yes.'

'And?'

Milly laughed. 'He's going home tomorrow.'

'Oh, no.'

'But we're having a meal out tonight.'

'Where?'

'My choice. Where do you think?'

'Not the Red Rose? Oh, Milly, that's hardly romantic. David gets so stuffed he can barely get undressed.'

'George, I've got to go.'

'No you don't. What are you going to wear?'

'I'm going into the Tube,' she lied before cutting the connection.

Milly sat in the Red Rose Indian restaurant with a complimentary glass of lager, feeling as relaxed as she could ever remember. She was wearing an old pair of jeans and her favourite linen Whistles top, with her hair tied back in a ponytail. When Mitch came in, she waved at him and a waiter brought him over to their table. They kissed, and he took a seat opposite.

'Any news?' she asked.

'No. I've been trying to get hold of Scott and Josie, but I couldn't.'

'Probably in meetings,' she offered.

'Yeah, I guess,' he said. 'Anyway, you look great. And if the food here tastes as good as it smells, I'll love it.'

Rocky, the restaurateur, appeared from the kitchen and bounded over to them.

'Milly, how good to see you,' he said.

'Rocky, this is Mitch. Mitch, Rocky.' They shook hands.

'You boyfriend, Mitch?' Rocky asked hopefully.

'No, Rocky,' Milly said. 'Mitch is a friend of mine.'

'Just a friend. Why?'

'Rocky!' Milly shrieked.

'Okay. Sorry. Sorry. Two Cobras. Yes?' he said before scurrying off.

'Rocky?' Mitch asked.

'Don't ask. He works too hard,' Milly said.

Mitch peered at his menu.

'Right. Chicken dope . . . ee . . . art . . . za.'

'Do'pee atsa,' Milly said expertly, a true aficionado of Anglo curry.

'That sounds Italian to me.'

'Well, it's not.'

'Okay. I'll trust you. You order for me.'

'Hello, Milly,' a voice bellowed from the direction of the door. Milly recognised it instantly and closed her eyes in disbelief before turning her head to say hello. It was her fault. She'd called Georgina, after all.

'Fancy seeing you here.'

Georgina looked at Mitch and halted for a split second, before letting herself smile broadly. Milly knew exactly what the smile meant. Any number of variations on the theme of 'Oh, Milly. You lucky bitch.'

'Mitch. This is my friend Georgina and her husband David. This is Mitch.' They all shook hands.

'Mitch, I've heard ever *so* much about you.'

Milly squirmed.

Georgina's intention had been to pop in for a takeaway so that she could cop a look at Harrison Ford Jnr, but it seemed she was now having a last-minute change of plan. David could sense that she was angling to join the happy couple, but in spite of his best efforts it didn't appear that he was able to shift her along. Actually it was quite comic to watch. It reminded Milly of her dad trying to take his old labrador for a walk when it was raining.

'Right, well, it was nice meeting you . . .' David said in an attempt to conclude their conversation.

The restaurant was busy and Georgina looked around at the full tables. Milly rolled her eyes, half expecting what was coming next. Mitch was American. He was too polite not to!

'Would you like to join us?' he asked, taking up the slack Georgina had so kindly provided.

'No,' David said definitively.

'Don't be so rude, David. That would be lovely.'

Mitch was enthralled by the sizzling chicken tikka that was placed in front of them, with its pungent aroma. It had taken him a while to get over the beer bottles being almost the size of wine bottles, and he was having an equal struggle with the mass of food that was at first placed, and eventually piled, on to their table.

'My God. Are we expecting any others?'

'David always orders too much.'

'What we don't eat we can take home,' he protested.

'Yes, but we never do, darling. It's always just mush.'

'Wow. This is wonderful,' Mitch said as he took a mouthful. 'Hey, never mind this script. I should take Rocky back to Hollywood with me.'

'It's not Rocky you should be taking back with you, Mitch,' Georgina joked, and everyone politely laughed, although of course it wasn't meant to be a joke at all.

Willenheim was incandescent. This ridiculous situation had gone on for far too long, and the only person who could answer any of his questions was pussying around in London. Willenheim had had enough.

'No one told me that he just had a fucking option agreement. That ain't worth shit. Columbia will change the title and, bang, they've got a new freakin' movie.' He hurled the document at Jerry Greene, who was sitting next to his boss, Dylan Tizer.

Jerry picked it up nervously. 'I was as surprised as you. Mitch led me to believe that he had a complete contract, assigning full—'

'Led you to believe! So you hadn't *seen* anything! And you're a *lawyer*!'

Willenheim crashed his considerable fist down on his desk. 'Carmichael is finished at this studio! Who the fuck does he think he is? And you're hanging by a thread, Greene.'

Jerry could feel his eyebrow twitching and he wondered whether Willenheim could see it also.

The door opened and Dolores walked in.

'I've just spoken with Josie, one of Mitch's assistants,' she began.

'And . . . ?'

Dolores paused. Willenheim knew then that she was about to deliver bad news. 'She's spoken with him today, but she doesn't know when he's coming back.'

'Well, then, why do I bother fuckin' payin' her?' Willenheim raged.

'Why indeed? Why do you bother paying half the assholes in this studio?' Dolores looked at a squirming Jerry.

'So fire her ass. Make me feel a little better at least.' Dolores looked thrilled at the prospect, and left with alacrity.

Jerry was now convinced that his twitch was there for all to see. His eyebrow must have looked like an epileptic caterpillar.

'So, Greene,' Willenheim said, 'what am I to do? Well? Do I have to remind you again that you're the lawyer on the job?'

'No, sir.'

'Well what the hell are you doing here then? Don't just sit there staring at me! Get your fat ass over to London, you dumb schmuck!'

'What? Now?'

'No, you fuckin' idiot, next month. Of course now.'

'Yes, sir,' Jerry said as he hurried out of the office with one clear mission in mind. He was going to kill Mitch Carmichael.

Jonson was having a great time in LA, with a generous expense account and no work to do. Life didn't get any better than this. It was as if all his dreams had come true. In his own inimitable style, he had made friends with most of the hotel's staff and half of its guests. A few white lies here and there, the odd exaggeration and embellishment, and Jonson was the English hero of the Holiday Inn. The staff could roughly be split in two. Half were full of vitality and hope, fully expecting their big Hollywood break tomorrow, and the other half were bitter, wizened old soaks struggling to come to terms with the fact that they'd missed the fame boat.

Now he was relaxing on a rooftop recliner, savouring the sun's rays and his good fortune in equal measure. He'd just swum several lengths of the pool and was flicking through a newspaper. A face leapt out at him. He'd seen it before but he couldn't remember where. The caption underneath didn't help. He racked his brains as he tried to recall how he had met a guy called Albert T. Willenheim, the head of Pacific Studios.

Everyone waited to see Mitch's reaction as he tried David's curry. He wasn't about to back down from the 'hot dish' game. He slowly chewed the chicken vindaloo and they all waited for the inevitable. It didn't take long. He narrowed his lips before starting to blow out rapidly, and then began wafting his hand in front of his mouth between glugs of lager. David and Georgina thought it was hilarious, but Milly felt sorry for him. She knew from bitter and burning experience the perils of quenching the curry fire with lager. A false sense of security if ever there was one.

'Shit . . . Now I know why the beer bottles are so big. What the hell is that?' Mitch asked.

'Vindaloo,' David announced as proudly as a dad holding his firstborn.

'Milly. Do you mind?' Mitch said as he reached for her beer glass.

'I'll get you some water.'

'Thinking ahead, eh, Milly?' Georgina's smile was wiped from her face by the scowls from Milly and David.

The graduation up through the Indian menu from korma to vindaloo was a scenario played out in Indian restaurants up and down the country probably every night of the week. Those reaching the vindaloo zenith each received a metaphorical certificate to hang at home, presumably in their toilet.

David said, 'You see, Mitch, you can't come straight in at vindaloo. Takes years of dedicated training. Two curries a week, for three years at least. That's what university is in this country. Anyway, have you enjoyed your stay in London? I hear Milly showed you the best sights.'

'Not all of them,' Georgina whispered.

'Well, it's been good and bad, actually. It's certainly been eventful, I can definitely say that. Lots of lows, but some highs as well.'

'When are you going back?'

'Tomorrow some time. Got to face the music.'

'Not totally empty handed, I hope,' Georgina prompted him.

'I've given Mitch a copy of my script to take back with him,' Milly said.

'Oh, great. Well, you'll love it, Mitch,' David said. 'I think it's fantastic.'

'Yeah, okay,' Milly said, blushing.

'No. There's no time for false modesty here. It's bloody great. You'd do well to read it, Mitch.'

'I will. I'm looking forward to it.'

Mitch excused himself and made off in the direction of the washroom.

'Oh, Milly, he's gorgeous.'

'George, I don't believe you,' Milly said.

'No, he is. Honestly.'

'Joining us. Tonight.'

'Oh, I had to see him. You'd have done the same.'

Milly smiled. 'So you approve, then?'

'See what you mean about the young Harrison thing. Totally gorgeous. And nice arse as well.'

David, who'd been enjoying his high male status after his victorious curry showdown, was now feeling alarmingly threatened by this lust fest. 'Oh, come off it. He's not that good-looking.'

'Oh, leave off, David. He's as horny as hell, okay? Just live with it.'

'Yes. Thank you, Georgina,' he said scornfully. 'Well, Milly, I think he's a really nice bloke . . .'

'Nice! Hah. Who cares if he's nice! David, you thought your curry was hot.'

'I'm just saying.'

'Oh, you're just jealous.'

'Actually, it's not me who's jealous, Georgina.'

'Hey, come on, you two. You shouldn't be arguing over him. You're not even in the frame.'

'He's a lovely bloke, Milly. And that's what's important,' David said.

'Can't you go with him?' Georgina asked.

'Hardly. I've only just met him, and aren't we all being a little bit presumptuous?'

'Well, I believe in love at first sight,' David said.

'Oh, that's nice, David, thank you,' Georgina responded, totally misinterpreting what he'd meant, but he wasn't about to correct the newly pregnant love of his life.

'He definitely likes you, Milly.'

''Course he does. He's hardly looked at me all night. What more proof do you need?' Georgina said flippantly.

'Perhaps he'll take you back to Hollywood. Make you a star writer. I can see it now. The winner of the Academy Award for best screenplay goes to . . .'

Georgina started drumming on the table with a couple of forks.

'. . . Juliet Millhouse.'

Mitch arrived back at the table to catch them all laughing. He had the timing of a comic on-stage for the first time. If he hadn't been so fastidious about hygiene he might have caught David's wry comment and solved all his problems there and then. In fact he missed it so narrowly he might live to rue just shaking the wretched thing.

'Wow. So what have I missed, then?' he asked as he sat down.

'Oh, nothing,' Milly said, embarrassed, hoping that neither of them would repeat it.

The restaurant was almost empty by the time Mitch signed his Amex chit. It was almost twelve o'clock, almost the next day, the day he'd be leaving, and it wasn't lost on either of them that another crunch time was upon them.

Mitch's mind was elsewhere as he signed his Amex chit at the Red Rose. He'd had another wonderful evening with Milly, and didn't want to fly home tomorrow. He had nothing to look forward to, probably didn't even have a job. But he had to go back. Maybe I'll get lucky, he thought. Heaven knows, he was due some luck. Before then, though, he had more pressing matters to take care of here. He wished he'd never met Milly, because what had started – and he felt sure something *had* started – was bound to end painfully. He knew how he wanted to spend the rest of the evening, but it wasn't as simple as that. It never was when you cared about the other person. Once more he went over the arguments for and against a night of unbridled passion. He decided that it would probably be best for both of them if they said goodnight now.

However, by the time he'd got out of the restaurant, he had completely changed his mind. There was nothing wrong with inviting Milly back for a nightcap and they could take things from there. If it went where he hoped it might and the venue was a problem for her, he would check out and into another hotel. One that didn't frown on two adults doing the most natural thing in the world.

'Milly,' he said, 'what do you wanna do now? I was wondering whether you might—'

His mobile shrilled. Mitch sighed. A call so late in the evening spelt emergency.

'Hello?'

'Mitch, it's Scott. I'm sorry to call so late . . .'

Whoever was phoning, Milly thought, they didn't have good news to impart. Sure enough, Mitch's haunted expression returned. The one she'd seen at the police station.

'Shit . . . the bastards. Why? Did they not give a reason? Have you spoken to her?' He was now pacing up and down angrily. 'What? . . . Yes. Well, it must have rung but we didn't hear it . . . Scott, there's no point us arguing about my whereabouts . . . Yes. I'll call him in fifteen minutes . . . No. Yeah! Get me on the first flight out. Call the hotel to let them know. I'll be there in twenty minutes or so . . . Come on, Scott, I don't give a shit what class. They can put me in the hold if they want to. Where are you now? . . . What? Jerry's coming to London? Why? . . . Well, that's fine, let him come . . . No, don't tell him.

Let him have a wasted trip. Where can I get hold of Josie? Hang on, hang on.' He gestured to Milly for a pen. She fumbled in her bag and passed him one.

'Thanks . . .' He scribbled down a number. 'I'm gonna call her. In half an hour or so, as long as it takes me to get back to the hotel, after I've spoken with Willenheim . . . Yeah, sure I'm gonna call him. Why shouldn't I? I don't see that I have much to lose.'

Mitch ended the call. So much for them spending the night together, Milly thought.

A cab stopped at the lights just ahead of them. Mitch flagged it down and Milly tried not to burst into tears.

'They've sacked Josie,' he said. 'It's all my fault, everything is, and I've gotta try to get it straightened out. She's just a kid starting out. Milly, you understand that I've gotta do this? Come here.' He held out his arms and they embraced. She buried her head in his chest. Mitch held her tightly, as if he couldn't bear to let her go. 'Milly, I so wish we hadn't met like this. I think you're the most wonderful person I've ever met, but this is a bad time for me now and I don't think I should be starting anything here that I can't see through.' She didn't say anything, just held him. 'Perhaps in a few weeks,' he continued, 'or however long this thing takes, you might come out to LA, or I could come back to London – I could get a job at the hotel.'

His joke didn't work, but she laughed anyway and they broke apart. It was no good trying to hide her tears now: they were there for all to see and she didn't care. They embraced again.

'I ain't got all night, mate.' The cab driver called out.

Mitch marched over to the cab and put his head through the window. 'Put your goddamn meter on and shut the hell up. Can't you see I'm busy here?'

He returned to Milly, and put his hands on her shoulders. He looked into her green eyes and then he kissed her. A surge of energy raced through her body like a ball bearing in a pinball machine, nearly buckling both her knees in the process. 'Milly,' he said, 'this is awful for us both but, believe me, you haven't seen the last of me.' They kissed again, then he got into the cab and drove away.

CHAPTER FIFTEEN

A cab pulled up at the corner of 42nd and 34th in downtown Hollywood. 'That's it over there, buddy.' The driver pointed.

'Thanks, mate, keep the change.' Jonson handed the driver ten dollars, which amounted to a thirty cents tip.

Pacific Studios was as impressive as Jonson had expected. He didn't know what he was doing there, but the fact that he happened to be in LA and knew Pacific's president was too good an opportunity to let pass. Milly would never forgive him if he didn't try to help her up the slippery pole. And, besides, as he was the inspiration for her screenplay, he felt an extra responsibility to do all he could. The task facing him was enormous, worthy of *Mission Impossible 3*.

Your task, he thought, should you choose to accept it, is to circumvent the heavy security presence, then blag your way past the Willenheim wannabes who have been employed specifically to prevent people like you getting in his face. Once inside the great man's office, you have exactly thirty seconds to extol the virtues of a literary nobody before a musclebound ex-football player turned bodyguard jumps repeatedly upon your head.

Jonson did what he usually did when faced with such insurmountable odds. He smiled.

The security guard's suspicions were immediately alerted: Jonson had approached his booth on foot. In all his twenty years in the job, no one had ever approached on foot. 'What can I do for you, son?' he asked.

'I'm here to see a Mr Willenheim. He's the president.'

'Oh, is he? Thanks for pointing that out, son. And you're here to see him?'

Jonson was unsure whether the bloke was taking the piss. He nodded anyway.

'Do you have an appointment?'

'I'm a friend of his.'

'Of course you are. Same country club, right?'

He was definitely taking the piss.

'Er, no.'

'And you are?'

'Jonson Clarke.'

'Well, Jonson, Mr Willenheim isn't expecting anyone today. So . . .'

'Will you just call him, and tell him it's me? The black guy from the plane. I sat next to him on a plane once.'

'Oh, you did?'

'That's right. And we became friends. And he said if I'm ever in LA . . .'

'Fuck off, dude. Go on the tour like everyone else.' The guard's patience had run out.

Clearly, Jonson thought, he wasn't going to get far with honesty, although he couldn't think of any alternative. A lesser man might have given up, but that didn't cross his mind: he had a tour to take.

He entered the studio-tour reception with a renewed sense of purpose. There was no one behind the desk and no prospective clients were waiting. It was quiet, apart from the hum of an air-conditioning unit battling against the Californian sun. The walls were decorated with posters of movies, past and present, including one for Eddie Murphy's *The Nutty Professor II*. Jonson was a committed Murphy fan. It amused him now that people at the airport had mistaken him for the star and he began to wonder how Eddie, or one of his characters, might handle his current mission.

A woman appeared in a corridor and began to walk slowly towards the desk with a Styrofoam cup of something steaming. Surely she couldn't be the tour guide; it'd take bloody ages. 'The next tour ain't till 'safternoon,' she said.

'I ain't here for no tour lady,' Jonson barked, in his best Eddie Murphy accent.

The woman looked up at him, startled.

'Shit, man, I'm Jonson Clarke, Mr Murphy's personal assistant.' He pointed to the poster.

'Oh.'

'Did Cindy call?' Jonson asked. 'Cindy didn't call . . . Ah, man, shit. Cindy should have called. I hope there ain't going to be a problem here, because if there's gonna be a problem, then I've got a problem with that. And I don't *want* there to be a problem. Do you? No. You see, lady, no one here wants a problem. All I wanna do is leave off the contract. That's it. Now tell me there ain't gonna be a problem.'

'Well. You could leave it with—'

'I ain't leavin' it with no one. You see, that's a problem. Right there, that's a problem. And, like I said, I ain't dealing with no problems. Uh-ah. I gotta give it to someone. And I mean physically give it to someone, and not just anyone either. It's gotta be the right person. That way, I'm covered, they're covered. Mr Murphy's covered and you're covered. Everyone's covered. We're all covered. All covered for *The Nutty Professor III*.'

'But why are you here? Shouldn't you be at the front desk? Perhaps they have your name.'

'Lady, this is a hundred-million-dollar picture,' Jonson rattled on. 'I don't care which door I use. You could beam me in for all I care. That ain't a problem. Contracts are expecting me and I don't think they'll care either which door I use. All that matters is that I do use a door and they get the contract.'

He must have been convincing because the woman picked up the phone as if her job depended on it. A satisfied and somewhat smug Jonson looked up at the poster again and winked. Mr Murphy should be worried: he had competition. Jonson hadn't realised until now just what a towering acting talent he himself was, and it made perfect sense that he should star in Milly's movies. Now, he had even more incentive to complete his mission.

Good fortune smiled on him, because anyone of any significance from the contracts department was in a meeting, and a hippie student called Lance had been left in charge to answer the phones. He was only working there because his dad just happened to be a movie director.

'Hello. Yes, Contracts?' asked the woman on the desk. 'Yes, Studio Tours, that's right. I have a Mr Clarke here from Mr Murphy's office, and he has the contract for *The*

Nutty Professor III script. I'm sending him right up.'

Lance put the phone down in disgust.

'*Nutty Professor III*. Don't these people have any shame?'

'I'm sorry about all this, Mr Jonson,' the woman said, as she rapidly filled out a security tag. 'If you take this and go down the hall you'll come to a little foyer with some elevators. If you wait there, someone will come and meet you.'

'Thank you, ma'am,' Jonson said, and set off down the corridor. He figured he had a matter of minutes before security guards were alerted to the fact that an unauthorised man was wandering around their offices. Uppermost in his mind was that all American security guards and most civilians were heavily armed: he might get himself shot. Milly had better appreciate this.

An urgent-looking little woman, carrying a bundle of papers, came scurrying towards him.

'Sorry to interrupt, ma'am,' Jonson flashed his security tag, 'I'm looking for the offices. I have a package for a Mr Willenheim.'

Her eyes widened. 'You'll need his executive suite. Fifth floor.'

'Thank you, ma'am. Much appreciate it.' It was a phrase he'd learned since he'd arrived on the West Coast.

Dolores looked at Jonson contemptuously. He expected her to ask him a question, but she didn't. She just looked at him. All his confidence drained out of him and he decided there and then that his acting days were over. They'd been fun while they lasted, and they'd served their purpose. 'Hello. I'm Jonson Clarke from England,' he said.

'Should I be impressed?'

Was he imagining this or had he stumbled into the office of the rudest woman in the world? Jonson's charm was called for and he gave Dolores his magnificent smile.

'What are you – a smileogram?' She scowled.

The smile vanished. 'Is this Mr Willenheim's office?'

'No. It's my office. What do you want?'

'I'd like to see Mr Willenheim.'

'Oh you do. And you thought you'd just stroll in on the off-chance he might be here.'

'Is he?' Jonson asked.

Dolores picked up the phone and hit a button on a console that Captain Kirk would have been proud of. 'Hello, Security?'

'No, no, I'm a friend of his,' Jonson interrupted.

Dolores smirked. 'Hold the line one second.' She looked up at him.

'I sat next to him on a plane a couple of weeks ago.'

She thought for a second. 'From London?'

'Yes.'

'Business class, right?'

'Yes. That was me,' Jonson said proudly.

'He mentioned you.'

'He did?'

'Yeah. You annoyed the shit out of him. Security, get your asses up here, I've got this idiot . . .'

Jonson decided to make a run for it. He didn't know where to but away from the world's most scary woman was a good start.

'Come back here!' Dolores yelled.

Jonson sprinted down the hallway for the lift. He could see that the doors were closing, and he thrust his hands between them as they rammed shut. It took an age for them to open again and Jonson leapt in and began hitting the ground-floor button continuously.

'Hey, buddy, relax, it's already lit,' said a voice from behind him.

Jonson hadn't been aware that someone else was in the lift and spun round with his fists up.

'What d'you want?' the man asked, cowering and looking terrified.

'What do you do here?' Jonson shouted desperately, as the lift started its descent.

'What?'

'Are you deaf?' Jonson roared. 'What is it you do here? What's your job?'

'I'm in Development. Who are you?'

'Do you know Willenheim?'

'Yes, of course I know him. He's the boss.'

'Can you get to him?'

The man couldn't answer. Jonson saw that he was paralysed with fear, but he had no time to explain himself. 'I need to get to Willenheim,' he said, and fumbled in his pocket.

'Okay. But what can I do? He's gotta load of security,' the man stuttered.

They had just passed the second floor on their way down, and Jonson ripped his hand out of his pocket, clutching a pen.

'Paper,' he screamed, and the man frantically handed

him a scrap. He scribbled furiously. 'You need great movies, right?' he asked breathlessly.

'Yeah.'

'Well, then, you need great scripts.'

'Yeah,' the man said.

The lift stopped and the doors opened. 'Do yourself a favour, why don't you?' Jonson pushed the piece of paper into the man's top pocket as the doors slid open.

'Freeze and put your hands above your heads.'

Standing before them were three armed security guards. With his mission completed, Jonson's tour was over. As he was escorted from the premises, it wasn't lost on him that Mr Murphy's blags never ended this way.

Milly was now grateful that Georgina had gatecrashed her dinner date, because she had come home with her, just as she had done all those years ago when Elliot left. It had been a wonderful evening with a terrible ending. Milly was emotionally exhausted and inconsolable. It was obvious that it wasn't just Mitch's premature exit which was upsetting her.

'It's all so difficult, George. It really is,' she sobbed. 'Something has got to start going right soon. For a moment there it all seemed too perfect.' Neither of them really believed Mitch's intention about their meeting up again. These were the sand foundations on which all holiday romances eventually crumbled.

'It will, Milly.'

'But when, though? It's not just him. It's everything. At the very least I've got to change jobs, but to what? I can't go back to buying now. I've always got money problems and all I cling to is this silly film script.'

'It's not silly. Mitch is going to read it.'

'Yeah, exactly. But that's all it ever is. Me waiting for someone to read it. And even if he does, do you think that'll just be it? No, of course it won't be. It'll just be another three years of waiting like it was before.'

Georgina couldn't bring herself to disagree, and for once in her life she didn't know what to say.

'And yes,' Milly sighed hopelessly, 'it would be nice to meet someone, someone I actually liked again. George, you're pregnant now, which I'm thrilled about, you know that, but it's made me think about things. Like what the hell I'm doing and where if anywhere I'll end up.'

Georgina still hadn't thought of anything to say, and nor did she try. She just hugged her friend.

Mitch stepped out of his shower at 7.30 a.m. He'd had an awful night and was rapidly revising his idea to open an Indian restaurant in LA, although it occurred to him that it might help people to lose weight. The night before he had made a succession of depressing phone calls, then collapsed into bed having instructed the hotel that he wasn't to be disturbed. He'd left his mobile phone in the taxi on the way back, which he was quite pleased about – as least it wouldn't be able to disturb him. Throughout the night, he woke at approximately half-hour intervals to empty his raging bladder and quench his thirst by sucking on the cold tap. He laughed when he recalled one of his conversations with David in the restaurant.

'Why do you call it the tapsucker bhaji?'

'You'll find out soon enough, believe me.'

His flight was at eleven, and he'd ordered a car for eight. He picked at his room-service breakfast and spent half an hour or so writing a note to Milly, explaining how sad he was to be leaving. He gave her his contact details in the States, thanked her for a wonderful couple of days, and talked about them seeing each other again. He stopped short of saying how he really felt about her, not because he didn't want to raise her hopes but because he wasn't sure what he really felt. It dawned on him that he might already be in love with her, but that was too complicated right now and he wasn't thinking clearly at the moment. His bag was all but packed, apart from her script, which he put in a side compartment. He'd promised her over and over that he would read it and he hoped he might do so in a professional capacity and not just as a friend, or even as a lover.

'You're in early,' Lucas said.

'Yeah. Couldn't sleep,' Milly replied. It was a quarter to eight, and she glanced at her screen. What a relief! He hadn't checked out. She had to see him again, if only to wish him good luck.

'Are you okay, Milly?' Lucas asked.

'Yeah, I'm fine.'

But he must have picked up that she wasn't. 'You don't start till half eight. Go in the office, I'll have Halim bring you some coffee. And when *he* comes down, I'll give you a shout.'

She smiled at him. 'Thanks, Lucas.'

*   *   *

Mitch hit the ground-floor button. As the doors closed he studied himself in the mirror. He looked tired. He felt as if he'd aged ten years in the last three weeks, and he had nothing to show for it. The doors opened again and Mitch stepped out.

'Mr Carmichael,' the Spanish concierge called, and ran over to him. 'Thank God you're up, sir. Please, you must come with me.' He ushered a bewildered Mitch to his desk and riffled through a drawer.

'I tried to get you in your room, but you were not to be disturbed. You have messages. Your friend Scott called three times, maybe four. I told him to try your mobile.'

The phone on his desk rang. 'One moment, please, sir.' He picked up the phone, listened, then handed the receiver to Mitch. 'It is Scott again, Mr Carmichael.'

'Hello,' Mitch said.

'Mitch, where the hell have you been? Your room is not to be disturbed, and I've been calling your mobile'

'I lost it and I'm sorry. You can punch me later when I see you.'

'No, you can't. You're not coming back.'

'They've fired me already?'

'No, you klutz. I've found her.'

This was what Mitch had dreamed of hearing, but now that he had, he couldn't take it in. 'You've found her?' he repeated.

'Yes.'

'Juliet? Our writer?'

'Yes. Juliet Millhouse, the writer of *Untitled*,' Scott bellowed, 'and you're not going to believe this but she's right there in London.'

'Are you sure? How did you find her?'

'It was so weird. First up, I think I'm gonna get mugged by this black guy, then I think he's going to whack Willenheim, but he turns out to be your guardian angel.'

'Scott, what are you talking about?'

'He just wanted me to have her details.'

'Whose details?'

'Hers. Juliet's.'

'Who was he?'

'Dunno.'

Mitch was utterly confused. 'And he just gave them to you.'

'Yep. In a note.'

'Shit. Where was he three weeks ago? What does it say?'

'Here, I'll read it to you. "Seriously good screenplay. *Untitled* by Juliet Millhouse. London-based writer." And there's her phone number too.'

'Read me the number again.' Mitch was stunned. Scott gave it to him and he scribbled it down. The concierge had helpfully provided him with paper and pen.

'I'll call her now and then call you back.'

'You'd better. I'm waiting by the phone.'

'Thanks, Scott.'

Mitch cut him off, dialled Juliet's number and waited for it to ring.

Milly's mobile rang in her bag. She thought about not answering it then came to her senses. It might be Mitch.

'Hello?'

231

'Hello . . . er, is that Juliet Millhouse?' a man asked nervously.

It sounded like Mitch all right, but it couldn't be him. He didn't know her name was Juliet and, as far as she could remember, she hadn't said her name was Millhouse.

'Yes.'

'Juliet Millhouse, the writer?'

Milly's heart skipped a beat. 'Yes. Who's that?'

'I'm calling from Pacific Studios.'

'Oh my God.' She covered her mouth. Maybe something awful had happened to Mitch.

'Have you written a script called *Untitled*?'

She tried to compose herself. 'What did you say?'

'Are you the writer of *Untitled*?'

Was this some sort of joke?

'What?' she asked.

'*Untitled*. Have you written a movie called *Untitled*?'

Milly's mouth was dry. She'd never heard one of her scripts called a movie before. What on earth was happening? 'Yes,' she said.

'Oh, thank God, Juliet. You have no idea how happy that makes me feel. I've been searching for you all over,' the man babbled.

Milly was now thinking the unimaginable. Could this be Mitch? But that would mean that . . .

'I'm over in London right now from the States,' the man went on.

Milly's mind imploded. She couldn't make sense of anything that was happening. This means that it's *my* script everyone wants. It was a preposterous notion. And, anyway, how could it be hers? She hadn't sent it anywhere, and neither had Lyal.

'What did you say your name was again?' she asked.

'Oh, forgive me, I haven't introduced myself. I'm Mitch Carmichael, head of—'

Milly began to shudder with excitement. Somehow this really was happening. Lucas came into the office. 'Milly. Your American—' He stared at her. 'Milly, what's up? Has he hurt you? Because—'

She covered the mouthpiece of her phone, and held up her other hand to stop him. 'I'm fine, Lucas, thank you.'

She put the phone back to her ear. 'And where are you?' she asked.

'Well, I'm from Pacific Studios but—'

'No. Where are you now?'

'What, right now?'

'Yeah.'

'I'm in my hotel. The Shelton Tower, Park Lane.'

'In your room?' she asked.

'No. I'm in Reception.'

Milly was staring at him now through the open office door. 'Same shirt as last night, I see. Nice one,' she said.

Mitch spun round and his eyes locked on to her. His bag dropped and so did his jaw. She smiled at him.

'Milly,' he said into his phone.

'Mitch,' she replied. Her voice bounced off a satellite hundreds of miles away before his receiver picked it up not twenty feet from her. Suddenly he dropped to his knees and ripped open the side compartment of his bag. Still on the phone, he pulled out the envelope she'd given him and tore it open. Then he looked back at her.

They gazed at one another for a long moment, then dropped their phones and raced towards each other. They fell into each other's arms in the middle of Reception. Then they kissed. Guests and staff looked on tolerantly – with the exception of Mr Mahmood.

When they broke apart, Mitch said, 'You're Juliet Millhouse?'

'Yes. You should have asked.'

'I can't believe it!' Mitch kissed her again.

'Nor can I. How can it have happened?' she asked.

'I don't know. Who cares?'

She looked more beautiful than ever now, Mitch thought, watching her animated face dancing with energy. Her moist and shining eyes were filled with both hope and relief, and he realised for the first time that, through all of this, it was she who had been suffering most, even more than him. He held her tightly and looked admiringly into her defiant but deliriously happy face. She was a vision of total happiness.

'So it was your script all along. Did you send it to the States? How did Willenheim get hold of it?' he gabbled.

But it was all too much for Milly to take in. The same questions were thrashing about in her mind, too, although she wasn't even trying to answer them. 'Mitch. Do you know something?'

'What?'

'You've just given me the best day of my life.'

Apparently Mr Mahmood had seen quite enough. 'Yes. Thank you. Happy couple very nice. Perhaps we can do this elsewhere, pliss.'

'But, Mr Mahmood,' Mitch said, 'I've checked out of my room.'

Mr Mahmood chaperoned them into his office, and no sooner had he closed the door than they were kissing again.

After some considerable time they stopped and looked at each other. The questions rampaging through their minds weren't going to go away, and they had to try to make sense of it all.

'Mitch, how can this have happened?'

'I have no idea. It's so weird. This sort of thing only happens in movies.'

'How come you just called me now?' Milly asked.

'Scott phoned me with your number.'

'But how did he get it?'

'Some guy popped up in LA with your details.'

'*Who?*'

'I don't know, but I need to call him anyway.'

'Pliss go ahead,' Mr Mahmood said, gesturing to his phone.

'Thanks . . . Is that you with Venom?' Mitch asked looking at the photo wall as he dialled.

'Yes,' Mr Mahmood announced proudly.

'Wow. I thought they'd be dead by now.'

While Mitch was on the phone, Milly took the opportunity to call Georgina. It was a few minutes before her friend could take what she had to say seriously.

'So you're the writer?' she exclaimed.

'Yes.'

'Tell me you're not joking.'

'It's no joke. *Untitled* is the script he was over here looking for. Can you believe it?'

'No. So how did it all happen, then?' Georgina pleaded.

'I've no idea. But I need to talk to Mitch now. I've gotta go. I'll call you later.'

'No. Don't you—'

'George, I'll ring you back.'

Milly hung up and looked at Mitch.

'Sorted,' he said. 'Scott's getting a message to Willenheim's office first thing. I still have a job, and you, young lady, have a film deal and a row of green lights. Have you ever met Mr de Niro?'

Milly leapt into his arms again, squealing with delight.

'You have to come to LA.'

'When?'

'Today, of course.'

'*Today?*'

'Yes. Today. And that isn't a request. You have to save my hide.'

Milly pretended to think about it.

'Did you find out about the guy with my details?'

'Oh, yeah. Scott didn't get a name but he said he was a black guy from England with a flaky scalp.'

Enlightenment and joy hit Milly at once. Jonson Clarke, her oldest friend in the world, had just come through for her in the biggest way imaginable. 'Jonson,' she said. 'My oldest friend.'

'Huh. Your oldest friend and my newest. I've got to meet this guy.'

'You will. He's on his way home today.'

*　　*　　*

Mitch cancelled his flight and rebooked two seats for that night so that Milly could organise herself. What a difference an hour could make. He had been returning to LA empty handed to get fired, and now he was returning a hero with the genius, who just happened to be the woman he now knew unequivocally he was in love with. But *how* had the script got into Willenheim's hands in the first place?

Mr Mahmood agreed to an extraordinary week's leave for Milly. It was a special concession to her, but he suspected that she wouldn't be coming back. He also granted her the rest of the day off.

Back at her flat, the state of her bedroom ceiling hadn't bothered Milly at all as Mitch and she made love. He was in the shower now and Milly was towelling her hair. Georgina had phoned to say that she was on her way over and Milly had left a message on Jonson's mobile asking him to get to her place as soon as he landed. She didn't tell him why. She wanted that to be a surprise for him.

Then she had had the second-greatest telephone moment of her life – second only to that morning's conversation with Mitch.

'Hello, Muriel. It's Juliet.'

'Juliet, hi, I was about to call you. Great news. Lyal's read the script and he loves it.'

'Oh,' she said casually. What a turnaround. Had Muriel called to say this yesterday, Milly would have passed out.

'And so he should,' Muriel added. 'Oh, hang on, Juliet, Lyal's just come free. I'll put you through.'

'No, I haven't got time to talk to him now.'

'Well, he's just here.'

'Tell him I'm flying to LA this afternoon with Mitch Carmichael to have a meeting with Albert Willenheim.'

'*Albert Willenheim!*' Muriel sounded shocked.

'Yes. Mr Willenheim wants to buy *Untitled*. Would you tell Lyal that for me? And that I'll be in touch.'

'Wouldn't it be better if you told him that yourself?' Muriel sounded flustered now.

'No, I don't think so.'

Milly put the phone down. She wasn't going to sack Lyal because, as she'd already figured out for herself, all agents are the same, but it was definitely payback time. Over the years, Lyal had dumped a huge pile of grief at her door, all of which he was now going to have to take back.

Georgina arrived in a heightened state of excitement and insisted on hearing the whole story. Still no one could work out how the script had got into Willenheim's hands. They would have to wait for Jonson to put the last piece into the jigsaw – if he had it.

'What about when Willenheim was at the hotel?' Georgina asked.

'No way. I'd have known about it. And, besides, he would have said,' Mitch told her.

Milly's phone rang. 'That'll be Lyal,' she said jokingly. 'Let the machine get it.' The machine beeped and, indeed, Lyal's voice filled the room. Milly couldn't believe it.

'Juliet, hi. Sorry I missed you. Great news about Pacific. I knew we'd get it off the ground.' He was trying to sound relaxed, but failing. 'I'm thrilled for you, I really am. It's nothing less than you deserve, because it really is a great script. I thought it was a fantastic idea the minute you pitched it to me that day in my office.'

Milly groaned at his audacity. 'Lying worm,' she said.

'So I'll try you on your mobile. We do need to get together to discuss this, Juliet. So give me a call.' Lyal tailed off, ending his olive branch with a rather feeble, 'Speak soon.'

'That man is shameless,' Milly said.

'Exactly what you want from an agent,' Mitch added. 'Are you going to call him?'

'Yeah . . . eventually.' And both Georgina and Mitch applauded.

Claudia had a new job, but little to show for it. As with Mitch, all her searches for Juliet Millhouse had drawn blanks, and she was becoming angry and frustrated in equal measure. Monty Ross, her new boss, was also disappointed, but he could think of other ways for Claudia to make it up to him, and he was looking forward to that. The only good thing about Claudia's situation at the moment was that her mole at Pacific had informed her that they hadn't signed the script yet either. As a bonus, it seemed that Mitch was about to be fired. Her phone bleeped and she hit the console. Her assistant came through the speaker sounding excited.

'Claudia, are you alone?'

'Why?'

'Because I have a call for you.'

Claudia tutted loudly. 'Who is it?'

'Juliet Millhouse.'

Claudia paused. 'Oh, my God, *Juliet Millhouse*?'

'Yeah. She's calling from England. I'll put her through.'

This was it. This was the breakthrough for which she'd risked everything. He who dares . . .

'Hello, Claudia Ingle.'

''Allo.'

'Hello, is that Juliet?' Claudia asked.

'Joo-Leigh Mill'ouse. I believe you've got me script, *Untitled* . . .'

Mitch had tracked down the lovable Joo-Leigh and she had been more than happy to oblige him. 'Don't you worry, me old son. Ah'll lead 'er right up the garden parf . . . and it'll cost 'er 'n' all.'

It was now four o'clock, and their car was almost due to take them to Heathrow, but Milly was desperate to catch Jonson, without whom none of this would have happened. Mitch, too, was keen to meet the guy: he wanted to say thank you and shake his hand. The front-door bell rang.

'That'll be him,' Milly exclaimed. 'George, go and let him in.'

Georgina opened the front door.

'Hey, George,' Jonson said. 'What are you doing here? Is everything all right?'

He had had a cryptic message on his mobile from Milly, whose phone had been engaged ever since; Georgina had answered Milly's door and had disappeared without so much as a hello. It was all very strange. He stepped into the hall. 'Hello?' he said tentatively, and walked into the sitting room.

The looks on the faces of the people waiting there confused him even more. Milly looked most peculiar of all, Georgina wasn't far behind, and there was some good-looking bloke he didn't recognise. What the hell was going on?

'I'm not in trouble, am I? 'Cos if I am you'll have to bollock me later. I'm knackered. I've been in LA.'

'We know,' Milly said.

'I know you know. You got me the job, Milly.'

'Jonson, it was you, wasn't it?'

'What?'

'You went to Pacific Studios, didn't you?'

His eyes flickered. 'Is that what this is all about?'

Everyone nodded.

'They haven't been in touch, have they?' he asked.

Everyone nodded again.

'Blimey, I was only there yesterday. Nearly got beaten up doing it as well.'

'Jonson, they've bought my script.'

'These three big heavies, all with guns . . . *what?*'

'Pacific Studios have bought my film,' Milly said, as tears streamed down her face.

'You're joking. Tell me you're not joking,' Jonson said.

Milly put her arms round him and whispered into his ear, 'You're an absolute godsend, Jonson Clarke, and the best friend I could ever ask for.'

'But I only gave them your name,' he protested.

'Jonson, this is Mitch,' she said, and wriggled out of Jonson's arms.

'How you doing, man?' Jonson shook the man's hand. He knew Milly so well that he could see something was afoot on a romantic front. 'I see that you two have *really* met,' he added.

Milly's smile confirmed his suspicions.

'Jonson, I owe you one hell of a big thank-you, man.' Mitch clapped him on the shoulder.

'You do?'

'I'm the one who bought the script, which has basically saved my life.'

'And made mine,' Milly added.

'Huh. How come you bought it so quickly? I only gave that bloke Milly's name and number.'

'We were hoping you might be able to tell us that,' Mitch said.

Jonson was flummoxed.

'Jonson, tell us what happened in LA,' Milly demanded.

'The truth?'

'Yes.'

'Okay . . . Well, first of all my delivery job gets cancelled, so I'm killing time at the hotel waiting for a flight home, yeah? And I see this guy's face in the paper. Albert Willenheim.'

'He's my boss,' Mitch said.

'Oh, right, yeah, 'course. You work for Pacific, right?' Mitch nodded.

'Anyway, it says in the paper that he's the big cheese of Pacific Studios in LA, right? Which is where I am at the moment. But I'm looking at his face, and I'm thinking I know him from somewhere.'

'You'd probably seen him on television over there,' Mitch suggested.

'I thought that at first. But it was more than that. I'd *met* him, and I was racking my brains and then it clicked.'

'You've met Willenheim?'

'Yeah.'

'When?' Milly asked.

'On the plane to New York that time. The flight when I was supposed to be reading your script. I got upgraded to business class, yeah, and he was the bloke I was sitting next to. So . . .'

Jonson carried on with his story but no one was listening to him now. They were all too busy fitting in the last piece of the jigsaw puzzle. It slotted in perfectly and appropriately was a picture of Milly smiling brightly and looking like the happiest person on earth. Jonson *had* mislaid the script but somehow one of the most powerful men in American cinema had found it, read it and set in motion the most astonishing series of events in any of their lives.

At Heathrow airport, the flight for Los Angeles was called, but Mitch and Milly didn't stir from their comfortable chairs. First-class passengers could board when they liked, and Mitch explained that they had another twenty minutes yet. Plenty of time to finish off their bottle of Moët. Milly had left the Shelton Tower, Park Lane Hotel, but not for ever: she would return, but only as a guest – it was so handy for West End premières. Before then, though, the hotel would have its part to play in their saga. Jerry Greene was booked in for tonight, and Claudia was boarding a plane in LA bound for London at this very moment to meet Joo-Leigh in the Park Bar tomorrow morning. Milly held Mitch's hand and squeezed.

He squeezed back. This was definitely happening. It was real. Milly had made it.

Don't miss Dominic Holland's
hilarious new novel

THE RIPPLE EFFECT

Coming soon from Flame to
a bookshop near you . . .